# LOVE IN A SMALL TOWN

# LOVE IN A SMALL TOWN

### *by*

## WANG ANYI

translated by Eva Hung

— An Authorized Translation —

A *RENDITIONS* Paperback

© The Chinese University of Hong Kong 1988
All Rights Reserved. ISBN 962-7255-03-3

This translation first published 1988
Reprinted 1990

**Renditions Paperbacks**
are published by
The Research Centre for Translation
The Chinese University of Hong Kong

*General Editors*
Eva Hung    T.L. Tsim

Printed in Hong Kong

FOR CHAI

# Preface

Born in 1954 in Nanjing and brought up in Shanghai, Wang Anyi was sent down to Anhui province in 1970 during the Cultural Revolution. There she joined a local performing arts troupe as a cellist. In 1978 she returned to Shanghai, where she began her career as a writer. She first tried her hand at prose, and it was not until 1980 that her first work of fiction was published. In her own words, this new departure opened a flood-gate — scores of fictional works followed, and with them an almost instantaneous public recognition. She has since won two national literary prizes for fiction.

Wang Anyi is now acknowledged as one of the most promising young writers to have emerged in China in the 1980s; she is also one of the most prolific, having published six collections of short stories, three novellettes and three novels between the years 1980 and 1987. This impressive output is fuelled by her ability to write about almost any subject which interests her, by her keen powers of observation and her versatility. From intriguing and entertaining tales about the life of common folk in pre-Liberation days, to the quiet pastoral charm of "Bao Village" and the lyrical introspection of "Love in Beauteous

Valley'', she has clearly demonstrated her remarkable range as a writer.

"Love in a Small Town", first published in *Shanghai wen-xue* 1986 No.8, is the second of three novelettes, popularly known as the "Three Loves", written by Wang Anyi between 1985 and 1986. The other two stories are entitled "Love on a Barren Mountain" (*Shiyue* 1986 No.4) and "Love in Beauteous Valley" (*Zhongshan* 1987 No.1). Though "Love in a Small Town" is chronologically the second work in this triptych, thematically it can be considered the opening piece since it traces the relationship between two teenage dancers, while the other two stories are about the courtship, marital and extra-marital relationships between men and women in their early twenties to early thirties. Both "Love in a Small Town" and "Love on a Barren Mountain" are based on real life stories Wang Anyi witnessed in the Anhui performing arts troupe. Through the misadventures of the men and women in the "Three Loves", Wang Anyi explores the meaning of love and the spiritual strength of women in the face of major emotional crises. She comes to the following conclusion:

> Women are born to suffer and to be lonely, patient and humble. Glory always belongs to men; magnanimity is a male attribute. Would you believe me if I told you that through their endurance of loneliness and hardships, women have long surpassed men in terms of human nature?*

During the anti-bourgeois liberalisation campaign of 1987, though Wang Anyi was not mentioned by name, some accusing fingers pointed to the "Three Loves", condemning these stories as examples of how even "female comrades" had

---

*"The Man and the Woman, the Woman and the City", afterword to *Love on a Barren Mountain* (Hong Kong: South China Press, 1988).

degenerated into writing about sex. Nothing could more plainly reveal the die-hard attitudes in China that: 1. sex is a taboo subject; and 2. it is worse for women than for men to break taboos. Actually the three novelettes are, as Wang Anyi has repeatedly pointed out, about human nature, not sex. Be that as it may, to date the three novelettes have not been published in book form in China. However, a Hong Kong publisher has made them available to readers outside of China under the collective title *Love on a Barren Mountain*.

The present translation is based on the first published version in the magazine *Shanghai wenxue*. I must express my gratitude to Howard Goldblatt for bringing the story, along with other works by Wang Anyi, to my attention in December, 1986. I am also grateful to John Dent-Young, Janice Wickeri and Zhu Zhiyu for their help and suggestions at various stages of the metamorphosis of this translation. This is the first English translation of a major work by Wang Anyi, and I believe that it will not be long before English readers will have a chance of reading her other works.

Eva Hung
Hong Kong, August, 1988

# Love in a Small Town

THEY HAD BEEN TOGETHER since they were very young, dancing in the same ballet troupe. They both danced in "The Red Detachment of Women"; she was in the "Dance of the Little Soldiers" and he in the "Dance of the Children's Brigade". She excelled on pointe because of the amount of training she had in the propaganda team at school; she had worn through several pairs of ordinary cloth-shoes practising her pointe work, and when she finally switched over to flat-topped ballet shoes, she felt ever so light and sure-footed, as if she had been doing weight-training and had just discarded the sandbags tied to her feet. His waist and legs were particularly pliant and strong because he used to study with a teacher who was also knowledgeable in the martial arts; he could do *tours jetés*, somersaults, anything required of him. Bending backwards, he could stretch till his head touched his feet; in his *balancé* to the back, the tip of his foot would touch the back of his head. He was really good. She was then only twelve, and he a few years older, just sixteen.

Two years have passed. The excitement over "The Red Detachment of Women" has subsided, and the troupe is

rehearsing "On the Yimeng Mountains". A teacher from the
Dance Department of the Provincial Performing Arts School
has come to conduct a day's class with the troupe, and in just
one day's time has found out that they have destroyed their
physiques through incorrect training. They don't have muscles, just flesh with neither flexibility nor strength. The
teacher even pulls her to the middle of the studio and,
turning her around, points out to everyone her typically
deformed legs, hips and shoulders. And the problems are
indeed serious; she has thick legs, thick arms, a thick waist
and very broad hips. Her breasts are twice the normal size,
protruding like small hills, hardly like a fourteen-year-old's.
The whole troupe, under the prompting of the Provincial
School dance teacher, scrutinizes her body, and it makes her
feel awful. Naturally she is ashamed, and to overcome this
sense of shame she puts on a proud and disdainful look,
holding her head high, throwing her chest out, and looking
at others out of the corners of her eyes as though they were
beneath her.

At this time she is half a head taller than him. Something must have gone wrong with his body; he has just
stopped growing, and though he is eighteen, he still looks
very much a child. He can only perform children's roles,
and yet when he is in costume as a child, his face is obviously
that of a grown-up. In fact he looks much older than his real
age. If he weren't such a good dancer, the leaders of the
troupe would probably have to think twice about retaining
him.

Though neither of them is a principal dancer, they both
work hard. In the early mornings and late evenings they are
the only people in the studio. Even in cold weather they strip
down to flimsy practice clothes, and they don't have to come
near to smell each other's sweat and odour, at once sweet and

repellent. His odour is strong, hers no less so. Her roommates, young girls with limited knowledge of such matters,
all say she has B.O. and refuse to sleep in the bed next to
hers. She doesn't care, and even thinks: "Well, even if it is
B.O., you haven't got it. It's the things few people have that
are really precious!" But this is just a thought. She nevertheless feels a little sad, and a little inferior. What she doesn't
know is it has nothing to do with B.O., just a strong natural
odour. Sometimes when they take a break during practice to
catch their breath, they will look at each other and, breathing
deeply, she will say out of curiosity: "Oh, you smell like
watermelon." Then he will lower his head to one side, raise
his arm and sniff at his armpit, and reply with a laugh: "My
sweat is sweet; that's why in summer all the mosquitoes come
after me." And sure enough, there are tiny brown scars all
over his fair skin; traces of summer left there, never to go
away. And then he will exclaim in a surprised tone: "You
smell like steamed dough!" She, too, will raise her arm and
sniff at her armpit, and reply: "My sweat is sour; mosquitoes
don't like me." And her dark skin really is smooth, without
even the tiniest mark. They will both laugh, a little short of
breath, and then resume their practice.

They mostly practise on their own, but sometimes they also
help each other out. Her legs are not very turned out, and he
helps her loosen up. She lies on her back on the floor, draws
her feet up towards her buttocks and he pushes her knees
down until they touch the floor on either side. When she
finally gets up, a damp human shape is left on the red-
painted floor, its legs bent outwards exactly like a frog's. It
takes a while for this silhouette to evaporate. He practises
pirouettés round and round the silhouette, as if encircled by
an invisible wall, stopping only when the silhouette disappears into the floor-boards.

He wishes that he could grow a few centimetres taller, and has the notion that the elasticity of the tendons is crucial to this, so he tries hard to loosen up. He stands on one leg with his back against the wall and, stiffening the other leg, asks her to push it towards his head. She pushes hard, her face against the curve of his calf. He always stands against the wall at one end of the bar as they do this, and with time there appears on the white-washed wall a yellowish human form standing on one leg, never to go away. When she stands at that end with one leg on the bar to loosen up, she is face to face with this one-legged man, and she thinks it's fun to trace a line from one footmark to the other.

They practise diligently, he no taller for it, and she much rounder and fleshier. She's tall all right, yet far from slim. Time passes, and they are one year older.

This is a small town bounded by three or four rivers, with a very narrow road leading to the railway. The best thing about it is its trees — elms, willows, poplars, cedars, peach, plum, apricot, date and persimmon — all fresh and green. If you travel on a ferry coming downriver, you'll see this green delta with its luxuriant vegetation a long way off; as you come closer, you will see the houses of grey and red bricks; and coming still closer, you will hear the water-men singing their work songs in a quite unaffected manner. People in this town are used to drinking river water, and get diarrhoea every time they drink well water. The water-men's business is to deliver river water to the town folks. The water is transported in oil drums on large carts, and spills over now and then as the carts jolt along the bumpy paths. Ruts left by the cartwheels, some shallow, some deep, criss-cross the paths along the banks. As the carts rumble from one rut to another, the wheels hit against the sides of the ruts and the water-man's voice lingers on one trembling note, very rhythmical. Just as one cart trembles off into the distance, another announces itself as it comes along, and so it continues, as much a part of the town as the luxuriant woods. And then the ferry resumes its journey, leaving behind several dozen passengers and a dozen or so pedlars carrying baskets on shoulder poles. They cross the wobbly gangway to the bank, and then follow the earthen path to the main street.

Most streets in town are paved with stone slabs, polished by the feet of pedestrians, baked warm in the sun. It's really comfortable walking on them wearing cloth-soled shoes and feeling the heat under your feet. The shoulder poles bob up and down as the pedlars' feet flap on the stone slabs, each step evoking an echo. When the pedlars reach the main street, they put down their baskets, filled with chives, the first harvest of the year, so fresh that the morning dew is still shining on them. That day, nine out of ten households in town eat dumplings stuffed with chives, and the fragrance fills the streets. The baskets, emptied of chives, are filled up with fried snacks, and leisurely the pedlars carry them away.

A horse-cart rattles along the street, heading south to buy hay. On the cart a bed sheet is hoisted as a sail. The old horse labours on, head down, while an unbridled pony gallops alongside, joyfully shaking its head and flicking its tail, lifting its slim legs ever so high. At times it runs ahead, at times it lags behind, and at times it heads off in all directions. It knocks over an old lady's black-jelly stall, but nobody minds. They all make way for it and let it get on with its antics.

On some walls the white-wash has peeled off, leaving bare the grey bricks underneath. Big posters are pasted on these walls, billing films shown in the cinema and plays put on in the theatre. A cinema ticket costs ten cents, a theatre ticket thirty cents. In the cinema things are just projected onto the screen, though the actors are really good; in the theatre you see real people performing, but they are less accomplished, so the pricing is fair. In the evenings both play to a full house, just the right number of people to fill up both places, so it's quite perfect.

At night, when all the pedlars are gone and all the shops are shut, the street is pitch black; only the stones shine in the crystal-clear moonlight. Doors are shut, then windows are shut, and then even the lights are extinguished. Children begin to dream about the days when they will be grown-ups; old timers sit thinking, or relive the memories of their younger days. Those who are neither old nor young have another kind of pleasure, moving in the dark, planting the seeds of life. This time next year, the town will hear the wailing of new inhabitants.

Now, there is nothing but pitch black silence.

In the cinema, only the screen is lit up, and human images move on it, enacting the joys and sorrows of life. In the theatre, the stage glitters and dazzles, and real people take on fictional roles.

They never stop practising; they can't even if they want to. If they stopped, she would get even fatter and thicker, and he, because his body has refused to grow even one centimetre taller, cannot afford to gain the slightest weight as that would make him look even shorter. And so they continue to practise relentlessly.

But actually it's not all hard work; sometimes it can even be fun. Her figure has developed in such a way that she looks awful whatever she wears, and is clumsy whatever she does. It's only when she takes her clothes off, leaving only the leotard, that her proportions become more pleasing. When she is engaged in dance movements, movements uncalled for in daily life, a good feeling surges inside her. She looks into the mirrors around her, and thinks to herself: it's unfair to say I'm ugly, and it's unfair to say I'm clumsy. Drops of sweat roll down her satin-smooth skin, like pearls. Her hair, all wet, sticks to her long thick neck. It grows down low, extending almost to the point where the neck is joined to the back. The short hairs on her neck are always getting wet, then drying off, and as a result become all curly. When the sun shines on this curly hair, in profile she looks like a little lamb.

He, too, looks more lithe when he's in practice clothes. Besides, since he's technically superior to most people, what does it matter if his physique isn't perfect? When he tries out some really difficult steps, he experiences a sense of elation. He takes off his vest, revealing his extremely white but coarse back. Acne spreads profusely all over his face and his body; it is as though the nutrition he absorbs must have an outlet, and since he gains neither height nor weight, all the nutrition and energy go towards nurturing his spots, which are like small red beans, a sign of his youthful vigour. When the spots gradually subside, they leave behind small brown hollows like wells. His back, in particular, is full of such hollows, and strongly resembles the rough surface of a rock. Each brown well is filled with a drop of sweat, clear and transparent.

Sweating is like taking a shower; it cleanses the dirt from even the deepest recesses of the body. After sweating, one feels extremely relaxed and carefree.

There is only a small room with a cement floor for having a wash-down. It's right next to the pantry, and the pantry is right next to a water pump, so they can mix the right amount of hot and cold water and then carry it into the washroom and put it on a small cement platform. Under the platform there is a drain, and at the back of the door hooks for hanging clothes. That's all there is for furnishing. Both men and women use this room, and if the door is closed, one has to shout: "Anyone in there?" and the person inside shouts back: "Occupied." If it's a woman's voice from inside, the man outside turns back and waits till she finishes, and vice versa. Otherwise the person inside unhooks the lock and stands behind the door, and then locks up again when the person outside has entered.

When the weather is hot, this room is quite crowded, and arguments frequently arise. But in winter it's deserted. Since it is a windowless, north-facing room with no sunlight all day and nothing to keep it warm, it can be very cold. The unpainted wooden door is half open, revealing the naked cement floor, whitened with constant washing. If it weren't for the little pools of water left on the floor by the two of them taking turns to shower every day, the room would be even more desolate. He always lets her have her wash first, while she is still sweating from the exercise, so that she won't feel too cold, but still she dares not stay too long for she will soon feel the piercing cold. While he is waiting, to keep his body warm he continues practising, doing *grand jetés* around the room. Every time he comes to the north windows he seems to hear the sound of water splashing in the washroom. He can't help but see, in his mind's eye, water flowing down her smooth, broad back, then diverging into two streams, running down her elephantine legs until it reaches the ground and runs over the cement floor.

One day she didn't shift her feet throughout her washdown, and when he carried his water into the room he saw that, amidst the little pools of water on the floor there were two footprints, completely dry, left there by a pair of feet wearing soft rubber slippers. He stared at the footprints, and gradually he traced a pair of ankles, calves, knees, thighs, and

up he went, until it seemed that the whole person was standing in front of him. Before he realized it, his water had
turned cold.

The next day he bought her an apple-green plastic bucket,
remembering that she had complained about the basin being
too small, saying even two basins of water weren't enough
for a good wash. A bucketful should be quite enough, he
thought.

Maybe with more water, she enjoys her wash more, and no
more dry footprints appear on the wet floor. All the footprints are drowned.

The bucket, filled with boiling water, flattens into an oval
as she carries it in her hand. Sunlight shines through the
apple-green sides, turning the water a tender shade of green,
with a layer of pale green steam hovering over it. The water
in the bucket shakes as she enters the small, dark room and
disappears behind the unpainted and half-rotted wooden
door. The room is extremely dark, with neither window nor
lamp; only a narrow band of light seeps through from underneath the door. But there is some light on the bucket of
water, luminous, a most tender green. The water is scalding.
A dry, stiff towel gets soaked in no time. She lifts this towel,
saturated with hot water, and puts it over her shoulder. She
can feel the water running down her chest and back, like
hundreds of needles pricking her skin. She sucks in her breath
with a "schusch" and repeatedly dips the towel into the
bucket, and splashes water over her body. The water in the
bucket gradually diminishes, and the light dims. Now she
starts to put on her clothes. She pushes the door open; the
sunlight hurts her eyes like the touch of a passionate and
violent lover. She is so happy! The sight of him sweating and
still engaged in a continuous series of *grand jetés*, a dirty
knee-band wrapped around his blackened leg, moves her to

pity, and she generously lends him the bucket.

The next day, she takes the bucket he has returned to fetch water, but finds that he has not cleaned it after he used it. There is a little greyish water left at the bottom of the bucket, and on the sides a film of greyish particles. She is just about to tell him off, and then stops herself and stands in a daze. She tilts the bucket and looks around inside it. There are tiny particles in the greyish water too, and she can't help speculating what they might be — can these be flecks of his skin? She knows that not only sweat comes from the skin, but also that tiny flecks of skin are sloughed off; not dust or dirt, just flecks of skin. When she thinks of this she can't help resenting it. She fills the bucket with clean water, pours it away, and then half-fills it again before she starts cleaning the sides. The plastic bucket seems rough to the touch somehow; something which she can't wash away titillates her palm. No matter how dark the room is, every time she scoops water up in her palms she sees tiny particles in it, particles swimming about like playful fish. On this day, even after her wash-down, she still feels unclean, and her back feels itchy. So she keeps moving her shoulders and back muscles about in some rather unseemly gestures. Her roommates resent her the more for it; some probably suspect that she has lice or something, though she washes every day while they only go to the public bath once a week.

The women's public bath is exactly like the men's. It's a big pool, and bathers lower themselves into it much as dumplings are put into boiling water to cook. By afternoon the water becomes murky. Since the theatrical troupe enjoys a special status in town, on Saturday mornings, before the villagers come into town, the public bath is open to the troupe for two hours so the actors and actresses can have their wash first. The girls all bring their own wash basins and scoop water from the pool to wash themselves. When they are done, they walk out with their hair wet and hanging down, their faces glowing, and their dirty clothes in the basins which they balance on one hip much as the renowned ancient beauty Xishi did after she finished washing silk by the river. At the door of the public bathhouse the villagers are queuing, their faces dirty, their eyes gluey and their bodies shivering. They look at the girls in wonder and admiration, trying hard to imagine what a blessed, royal life they lead.

On winter afternoons, there are always men and women walking about the streets, their faces glowing from the heat of the public bath.

The men and women with glowing faces, carrying baskets on shoulder poles or in their hands, or pulling carts, are satisfied, and hurry along the roads leading out of town. One of these roads leads to the pier, another goes north across the flood-gate. In the evening the sun gradually sinks behind the three high red flags cut in the earth on top of the flood-gate, and turns these discoloured flags a deep red. This is the noisiest hour here below the gate; carts rumble past, interspersed with the solitary ringing of bicycle bells. Women wearing home-made shoes walking on the dusty cement road leave behind clear imprints of the even or uneven sewing on their soles. They hurry on while the sun is still shining. When they reach a dirt track, their footprints are lost in the shifting dust.

It is the dry season; it hasn't rained for three consecutive months. On the main road the loosened earth is a full inch thick, completely covering your feet as you walk. The fields are cracked, the ponds dry, the water from the wells murky, and the water level of the river below the dam has gone down, laying bare dark green moss. The setting sun is fiery. After sinking behind the flood-gate it stays, as if by magic, behind a small green wood in the distance. Every small wood is a village you can see but can't reach, like a mirage.

Deep in the night when all is quiet the dogs start barking in the distance. The dogs in town don't bark, but then hundreds of cats create a commotion. At times like this their screeching shakes the whole town; they seem to be crying, or laughing, or panting, or sighing, and no one is able to sleep. Some bachelor jumps out of bed, grabs a shoulder pole and hits at two cats blindly, trying to separate them, but they seem to have been glued together since birth. Looking closer he finds they're two silent dogs. The cats have all gone and are continuing their heart-rending cries elsewhere. The next morning the bachelor gets up with blood-shot eyes, curses the cats, then curses the dogs, and then looks up at the sky. It doesn't look like it's going to rain; he curses heaven. Lastly, he thinks of the couple from out of town who are staying in the secondary school; they actually wear pants with stripes and floral patterns. Though they only do it in the house, at bedtime, still pants are pants; how can you have stripes and flowers on them? It's just not right.

They have worked diligently through a severe winter, and have now seen the coming of a dry spring. Her body is so rotund that it's impossible for it to grow anymore; it's like a ripened fruit, but the proportions are wrong. And his body seems as stubborn as his will; it is fixed, refuses to grow. Though she looks like an adult she is still very childish. She never hides her feelings. She will be laughing one minute, crying the next, as changeable as the summer weather, and yet you don't feel that she's abnormal or affected, simply naïve. When a group of girls goes on and on teasing a boy in the courtyard, and finally gets him to say: "At night my dad bites my mum's mouth", the others all laugh to themselves but pretend not to have heard and change the subject, while she falls about with laughter, completely losing control of herself. It's not only that she doesn't cover up for herself, she nullifies the others' efforts at evasion. They all turn red and try to stop her, but then she says, seemingly very knowledgeable: "The child knows nothing." The others just don't know what to make of her, and can only call her "Silly girl!" But she won't even put up with that, saying in protest, "Who says I'm silly? I know everything." All they can do is ignore her. As she grows more and more like a woman, her childishness and clumsiness become more apparent.

She still asks him to help her turn out her legs and loosen her joints, just as she used to when she was young. Though this task has become more and more difficult for him, he can't turn her down, and it has become a torture for him.

She lies before him, her legs bent in front of her chest, and slowly parts them to either side. He can't control the turmoil in his heart. He is panting loudly, almost suffocating with the effort to suppress himself. Sweat pours down from his head, his face, his shoulders, his back and from the inside of his thighs. As though to compensate for his child-like body, he has matured mentally with unusual speed, and he feels like a completely adult man. When he helps her to loosen up an evil thought takes hold of him; he wants to hurt her, so he pushes hard. She screams; a scream like the siren on a ferry.

It frightens him; his hands weaken, letting go of her knees. She brings her knees together, and holds them in her arms in front of her chest, still screaming. Then she starts to revile him, using a whole series of dirty words which only men would have used, such as "fuck you". She doesn't really know what it means, just that it's a strong word and gives vent to her anger. This, however, works on his imagination and makes him more agitated, so he throws the same vulgarity back at her, only he means it. She still doesn't understand its meaning, and still lies on the floor holding her knees in her arms. Nor does she hold them properly; she holds onto one knee and stretches the other leg, and then she holds onto the other knee while stretching this one. Every time she stretches or bends her legs her well-developed waist and chest vibrate in response. As he swears back at her, her anger mounts, and a string of dirty words such as "fuck your brother-in-law" come out of her mouth, illogical and unfit for any ear. He gets worked up, and counter-attacks in even coarser language, meaning every word of it. She won't let him speak anymore, just continues her abuse in a loud, shrill voice, trying to drown him out. His voice is deep and strong; it comes through gradually. When she thinks she has won and stops to catch her breath, his voice is still resounding in the room. Only then does she realize that he has not stopped cursing, but has kept up with her. His voice is like the bass in an orchestra; it may not carry much of the melody, but it always has a part to play. She doesn't even have time to catch her breath before she starts cursing afresh, trying to best him. He doesn't give up, and follows her shrill clamour with his deep, deliberate voice until she is finally exhausted and starts to cry, rolling all over the floor. He then stops, and stares at her gloomily.

Her whole body is blackened with dirt, and she rubs her eyes with her blackened hands so that her tears become black too, and roll all over her dirty face. Suddenly he feels sad. He takes her bucket, fills it with warm water and tells her to have a wash. She refuses to listen and goes on crying; this show of sympathy makes her cry even more pitifully and she feels even more heart-broken. All he can do now is go forward and pull her up. Though she's heavy and is deliberately clinging to the floor, he is extremely strong, and has no trouble getting her on her feet and pushing her into the washroom. When he hears her locking up and then sobbing in the midst of splashing water, his heart is suddenly filled with love and tenderness.

Her heart feels lighter as she splashes water on her body and feels the dirt and sweat wash away like a layer of unwanted skin. By now her tears have dried, but she goes on sobbing as though in protest. Yet at the same time a strange feeling of warmth fills her heart, gradually spreading throughout her body, like the gentle touch of someone very intimate. She is almost happy, but she doesn't want to stop sobbing, for this, too, seems a consolation.

From this day on they stop talking to each other; they are enemies.

Though they don't talk, they still practise. He practises on his own, she on her own; he doesn't help her turn out, she doesn't help him loosen up his legs, they just practise by themselves. They both look very grave, over-serious, as though attending a solemn occasion. There is no more conversation or laughter in the studio. When they laughed in the studio there used to be a slight echo, but now the only sound is the thump of their feet as they land on the floor, and the echo sounds empty, emphasizing the solitude and the monotony.

In contrast to this hushed atmosphere are the excitement and tension in their hearts. In her heart she is still contending fiercely with him, cursing him with hundreds of dirty words she doesn't understand. After that, she feels she is the one who has been abused, she who is pitiful and helpless, so she is more self-pitying than ever. Every movement is carried out in a long-suffering and dignified manner, and she doesn't realize her own affectation. All she feels is that there seems to be a fresh goal in practising, that it has become more meaningful. It is no longer just self-entertainment, nor just self-improvement, it seems to have taken on the added dimension of a performance. Thus she practises harder than usual, and becomes extremely demanding of herself. When she fails to execute a step she just lets go of her body and lets it flop heavily to the ground. The pain often makes her want to cry out, but she always holds back. She will struggle to get up and make a second, hopeless attempt. It seems that by doing so she hopes someone will be moved; actually she moves herself to the point of tears.

He, in the meantime, is also torturing himself, bending and folding his body into inconceivable shapes. He bends down, his head touching his feet, but he isn't satisfied with that. He sticks his head out between his feet and holds it erect so he can look at the world from the usual angle. The shape of his body becomes most perplexing; one can't even tell his trunk from his legs. But as a result of this 360-degree inversion, his eyes survey the world with greater equanimity. He can hold this position for twenty minutes. He seems to hate his body and is intent on punishing it; as if his body has an existence independent of and antagonistic to his soul, which is meting out the punishment. The punishment is so harsh that it becomes a little pretentious. Each, for untellable reasons neither of them understands, strives for excellence. Thus it comes to the time of the first spring rain.

The rain comes like this:

The prelude is hot, July-like weather. People haven't even had time to take off their sweaters before it becomes so hot that they don't want to keep their T-shirts on. Skirts appear in the courtyard, yet they don't have the courage to go outside; they just flaunt themselves ruefully on the premises of the theatrical troupe. All of a sudden the sky darkens; it remains dark for a whole day before it pours down, each drop of rain the size of a bean. Cool air descends as though time has reversed its journey. In a split second the colourful skirts are gone and the quilts laid out to air in the courtyard all collected, exposing the wet cement floor. The floor is uneven, the depressions hold water, and rain falling on these small pools ripples successive circles outwards. It is now evening, and a rainy evening gives one a feeling of warm desolation, or is it a cool warmth? The rain flows down along the tiles on the roof of the studio, clumsily following a circuitous route to the eaves. Soon there is a curtain of water hanging from the eaves.

There is a curtain of water in front of every house. People leave their doors half-open and, leaning on the door frames, separated by the water curtains, start chatting. The talk is all about the drought and the rain this spring. They eat as they chatter on, a big bowl of rice in the left hand, a pair of warped wooden chopsticks in the right, picking up the rice in the congee with the chopsticks. The congee looks a little brownish-red because of the sodium added, and seems the more tasty for it. There are a few salted beans and pickles in the bowl, smelling of mould, but once you're used to it the smell becomes quite delectable. The rain falling on the pebbled pavement makes a surprisingly loud noise, drowning out any other sound, so people have to shout. There is one house with its door locked: whoever lives there hasn't come home yet, and the clothes hanging out in front of the house have not been taken in. There is a pair of pants with floral patterns, all wet, and the flowers look exceptionally colourful.

It has turned cool again, and sweaters are called for. Villagers who have no sweaters wear quilted jackets, nearly all of them black. After the rain the streets actually seem a little desolate and cold. The pebbled pavement has been thoroughly washed; the earth looks darker and the pebbles brighter, as though outlined in ink. The water in the river has risen, and looks crystal clear, covering the moss on the banks. The cement path beneath the dam appears whiter than before, but the dirt track looks darker. The scattered woods are all fresh and green, like villages made up of trees. In one village, a child has died during the heavy downpour; he was going to the lake for weeds to feed the pigs, and slipped when he was walking by a catchwater. The story has spread over several miles and then vanished, as if scattered by the wind. The townsfolk still say that the rain has been timely, making the weather more pleasant, and the villagers are also singing its praises, for the green wheat in the fields has all brightened up.

They still don't talk to each other, as though they're deadly enemies. Others all notice it and think it strange. Yet after a while they become used to it and are no longer surprised. But after they've been used to it for a while, they once more feel that there's something strange about it. Since the animosity has lasted so long, there must be an unusual reason, and they can't just let the two of them be enemies forever. They have asked her, but she won't talk; they have asked him, and he won't talk either. They go back to question her again, and because they seem so serious, she can't help taking it seriously too, reacting in a stiff and stubborn manner. Her reaction draws even more attention, as they think that she is about to open up her heart, and they become even more persistent in their questioning. This rouses her feeling of having been wronged, which is further exaggerated because of their seriousness, and she bursts into tears. The fact that she is crying strengthens the confidence of others to get at the root of the matter, but she shakes her head in tears: "I don't want to say anything. I have nothing to say." It is the truth, but it sounds as though there is much behind it. They keep on questioning her, but then she refuses to speak anymore, just keeps crying as if she's heart-broken. She is crying partly because she feels she has been wronged, but more because she is puzzled and embarrassed as she knows for a fact that nothing has happened. Nothing has actually happened, and yet the situation looks so serious; she feels responsible, and therefore a little afraid. Her reaction at least partially satisfies the others. They feel that now they are justified in going to question him again.

Cornered, all he can do is hit back at them verbally. He is all tensed up, cursing ferociously; he doesn't know what he is saying or why he is saying it. He feels rather ridiculous but he simply can't stop. Everyone is shouting at him, telling him to stop, telling him to apologize to her. Apologize for what? They all seem to know; the two of them are the only ones who don't understand, and yet actually the two of them are the ones who do. But they don't realize this; they think that they understand nothing, and feel that they have been wronged, the victims of a terrible joke.

They are surrounded by the others, and the leader of the dance section grabs each by one hand, trying hard to make them shake hands and be friends again. Both of them are struggling fiercely and it takes the combined effort of everyone to hold them. She is crying, he cursing; both are angry and frustrated because they are struggling to no end. At last their hands touch; they are still struggling to avoid touching one another, but now the aversion seems a little false. Their hands touch, and they suddenly seem moved, the struggle to free themselves has obviously weakened. Their hands are at last brought forcibly together by the section leader, palm to palm. He has never felt more strongly about her body before, nor she his. Their hands touch for a split second, like lightning, and in the midst of everyone's resounding laughter their hands part, and they both turn to escape. But that split second seems so long, long enough for them to experience and savour for a lifetime. It is as though in that split second when they touch, he realizes that this is the hand of a woman, and she that this is the hand of a man. They escape, so ashamed that they can't look each other in the face, let alone talk to each other.

So it is that they still don't talk to each other. But now their silence has everyone's approval, and they are left alone. They practise as usual, and as hard. She throws herself violently on the floor; the physical pain gives her such a wonderful sense of satisfaction that she has become almost addicted to it. The more painful it is, the more she sympathizes with herself, and the more determined she becomes. He tries his utmost to twist his body into unrecognizable shapes, for that is the only way he can calm down; he is proud of his severity to himself. When either one of them leaves the studio, the other's determination and confidence in this self-torture will disappear, the physical tension and excitement vanish all of a sudden. They torture themselves because they want to show something off. It is a pity that they are concentrating so hard on themselves that they can't spare ten per cent, or even one per cent, of their attention for the other's performance. Their effort is completely wasted. Their need for the other person originates in themselves. There is satisfaction and meaning in hardship and endurance only if the other person is present. Yet ultimately both are showing off to themselves, hoping thereby to gain their own trust and sympathy.

But young and ignorant as they are, it is only natural that they don't realize this. They simply take delight in practice, and feel that they need each other's presence during practice.

Because of this inexplicable need, they have a tacit understanding: they won't practise alone, but if one of them comes
to the studio, the other will turn up unbidden, and once
there, neither will leave without the other.

After three heavy downpours, the weather bcomes hotter
every day; it is summer. The cicadas sing from before day-
break until night. The sun penetrates the thin tiles of the
studio roof and the heat surrounding the room pours in
through the open door and windows. Every day they give the
floor a thorough wash with their sweat, and the red paint
gradually fades, revealing the original pale colour. It is
wonderful to feel the sweat exuding through every pore. Her
wet leotard sticks to her body. She is practically naked, the
hints are so blatant, though not the tiniest part of her body
is bare. These hints, much more strongly than nakedness,
stimulate thoughts and desires. She is not well-proportioned;
every part of her body is exaggerated or distorted, like the
creation of a cartoonist. The curves thrust in and out without
restraint. Yet once you are accustomed to it, normal, well-
proportioned bodies actually seem flat and dull.

He is wearing nothing but a pair of athletic shorts and a
shabby knee-band round his left knee. He is so thin that his
bones seem to stick out of his pale, coarse skin; as he dances,
one can see his bones moving under his skin. His ribs are
clearly visible, two neat columns of them, giving the impression that the skin here has disappeared. His ribs, strong
as steel, obstruct the flow of his sweat, which either streams
down from rib to rib, or gets caught between the ribs, casting
a pattern of shadows on his body. Her body is as smooth and
shiny as velvet, with sweat pouring down. The two of them,
dripping wet, now turn their attention to each other and
really see each other for the first time. Before this the one has
never looked at the other; each only saw, admired and loved

himself or herself. Now, while they try to catch their breath, they suddenly have a chance to look at each other, and in the other's dripping body they seem to see their own naked image. They feel shy, and can't help avoiding each other's eyes. They are still resting; it is too hot and the cicadas are too noisy.

At mid-day, the only noise is that of the cicadas' song. Every front door along the street is open, yet no sound comes from the houses. People don't even snore during their afternoon naps; just trickles of saliva, still warm, shine and even steam on the pillows. The shopping hall in the department store looks especially deserted; there are only flies buzzing and tracing out circles in the air. The shop assistants are bent over the counters, fast asleep, the glass surface of the counters cooling their faces, and their faces warming and moistening the glass. Occasionally an untimely customer will hesitate in the shopping hall and glide noiselessly across the marble floor. No ferry calls at the pier; under the red-hot sun the river reflects a blinding light. Naked children walk a long distance along the banks and put their feet into the river to test the water; it's boiling. There are several water-carts lying around, with planks raised, and the water-men sleeping underneath them.

She tries a *grand jeté* in which one foot is supposed to touch the back of her head, but she fails, and falls heavily onto the floor. It seems as if it is the floor which rises up to meet her and strikes her a heavy blow. The feel of the warm floor boards suddenly makes her weak. She turns over, and lying on her back, arms outstretched, stares at the triangular roof of the studio. A thick strut points down at her body as though it is going to come crashing down. The shady ceiling is wide and deep, a sanctuary. She feels calm and untroubled.

Her eyes follow the ceiling's dark edge downwards, and come up against the unexpected glare of the sun. The sun's rays are particularly bright just beneath the eaves, and it makes her sad, almost hopeless. She lies on the floor, motionless, time flowing by her side, and stopping by her side. There is a tall, old scholartree in the courtyard, its leaves casting pale shadows on the window. She almost catches a glimpse of that ever-singing cicada spreading and folding its wings.

Just at this moment, two steely thin legs appear by the crown of her head; the leg bones stick out and all the muscles seem to recede rapidly toward the back. She cranes her neck backwards to look at these legs; there are some sparse, coarse hairs, pitch black against his snowy skin. She stares at them quietly, and finds them ridiculous. But now the leg bones are leaning towards her. He is squatting in front of her, looking into her eyes. He asks all of a sudden:

"Want me to give you a hand?"

"No!" She wants to shout, but her voice is hoarse and she can't raise it. With a quick push she sits up, but his hands are already under her arms, and before she can steady herself he has pushed her up to a standing position. She wobbles, but his hands grip her armpits like iron wrenches and force her to stand steadily. With his hands still under her arms, she feels the burning heat there, while other parts of her body have cooled down. The heat from these two places is overwhelming. She doesn't feel hot anymore, and the sweat flows down pleasantly, like a song. When she is firmly on her feet he takes his hands away and lowers them until they reach his thighs. His palms and wrists are all wet from the sweat in her armpits, and the warmth of her armpits envelops his hands. Now, his hands, hanging by his side, seem lonely and desolate. He can't help stretching his fingers, trying to catch something, but there is nothing there.

She is back on her feet now, and walks straight towards the
bar where she starts to do *balancé*, the tip of her foot drawing
empty semi-circles in the air. Bright sunlight catches on her
foot and throws half a halo in mid-air. The movements of her
protrusive, almost deformed buttocks seem so extraordinarily
displeasing to the eye that he really wants to kick at them. She
is conscious of his stare, and it makes her happy. His eyes are
warmly fondling her thick legs, legs which have lost their
elegant curve, and yet have an innocent appeal in their ugli-
ness. She continues her series of *balancés*, and feeling her
tendons stretch and relax she is so light-hearted and so happy
that she can't hold back the urge to glance at him. To her
surprise he has already gone back to his own routine. Her
spirits plummet; though her legs are still swinging back and
forth, her heart is not in it anymore. He is doing a sidesplit,
and as his legs form a straight line on the floor, he bends his
torso slowly to the front, with his arms touching the ground,
parallel to his legs, and his hands clasping his flexed feet. He
senses her attacking him with her stare, aimed at his weakest
and most sensitive spot. He can't help shivering, and folding
up his limbs he crouches on the ground. She has withdrawn
her stare. Dispirited, he curls up on the floor for a long while
before standing up again. Plucking up his spirits, he walks to
her side. He stands there struggling with himself, blushing.
Finally he mumbles:

"What is it that you dislike about me?"

She doesn't expect him to speak, let alone about something
so serious, so she too is embarassed. She gradually lowers her
leg, her face turning red. She answers: "Nothing," and
laughs as though it is funny.

"We'd better stop this," he says. "We should help each
other out."

"That's all right with me," she replies, her heart pounding. She feels this is something unusual.

And so they begin to talk to each other again. Yet somehow they feel that it was more wonderful when they were not on speaking terms. As soon as they talk to each other, the tension is gone, and then the sense of excitement, the inexplicable agitation and curiosity in anticipating the outcome of these events, and the secret flow of ideas by tacit understanding are completely gone, too. But still, they both feel that a weight has been lifted from their minds. The tension was just too great, and too dangerous. They did not realize what kind of danger it was, but they both felt the sense of adventure.

Their relationship has returned to normal, but they no longer have a clear conscience. Each seems to be harbouring secret designs; they avoid each other and no longer help each other practise. They talk, but only briefly and awkwardly. When he wants to tell her that the canteen has started serving and that if she's late she won't get any good dishes, he means well of course, but his words sound like a warning: "Meal's served!" And she answers angrily: "Who needs to be told!" When she has finished showering and wants to tell him it's his turn, she speaks as though it's an ultimatum: "I've finished, I'm telling you." And he replies, seemingly irritated: "Who needs to be told you've finished!" It seems that this is the only way in which they can talk to each other; they have forgotten how pleasant and natural conversing with each other used to be. Though they use angry words, they don't really quarrel because neither of them wants to do so. They don't want to be enemies again. Coming out of that embarrassing situation wasn't easy, and they treasure the break-through. But they both seem a little regretful that the embarrassment is over. Originally they thought that something extraordinary was going to happen, and they were full of expectations, a little afraid, a little hesistant. But now everything has returned to normal; nothing extraordinary will ever happen, or rather, something started to happen and then stopped, so that their expectations have fallen through and they feel strangely resentful of each other. The stiff way in which they talk to each other is thus not all pretense, there is some real cause for it. She frequently glares at him sideways for no reason at all, the whites of her eyes showing even more distinctly against her dark complextion, which makes the glare more effective. He looks as though he is always brooding; his face seems overcast, and since his complexion is pale this sense of gloom is all the more obvious. Sometimes it really scares her, and she dares not give full rein to her temper.

But still, they are on speaking terms again. Ever since they started talking again they seem less dedicated in their practice. Self-torture has lost its meaning, and when they look for a new way to communicate and to fight they can't find it. They are both at a loss. For a period of time they seem to have lost their goal in life and have become dispirited. Besides, the weather is extraordinarily hot. In the mid-day sun someone breaks an egg on a paving stone in the street and watches it cook. Almost a hundred people come to watch, their faces all sweaty and oily, but they are so amazed by the sight that they completely forget about the heat. Only the children keep on crying loudly because the prickly heat on their heads, all pus now, is hurting terribly. At night, though the sun is gone, the earth pants for breath from the heat it has soaked up, and exhales it in gasps, steaming the bamboo beds and straw mats lying all over the streets. Actually it is as hot outdoors as it is indoors, so hot that even mosquitoes don't come out.

Yet in the countryside the crops are growing particularly luxuriantly; the leaves of the beans are a delightful green and tender pods have appeared. Old villagers, like dogs, stick their tongues out in the heat but they still keep saying, "It's hot when it should be hot and cold when it should be cold; that's the way for the weather to be." The melons are growing nicely too. A small watermelon — thin-skinned, with red pulp and black seeds — only costs three cents. A pedlar carries them through the lanes and streets, shouting as he goes along. Even in the early morning one feels greasy because of the heat, so someone in the troupe beckons the pedlar into the courtyard and everyone sits around his basket eating melons. After they have eaten their fill they ask the accountant to pay the pedlar and charge it to the "heat-prevention" account.

The pedlar takes a rest in a shady corridor at the back of the kitchen, where there is actually a little breeze. He feels good and it makes him talkative, so he starts telling stories about the melon fields. These are all scandalous stories, such as the one about a farmer catching a couple fornicating while he was keeping watch in the melon fields, or a young girl who wet her pants from eating too many melons. Someone reports this to the troupe leader, and the pedlar nearly has to forfeit his earnings from the melons. Yet on the whole he has had an easy day; he has sold two basketfuls of melons without having to endure much of the heat. Now he has finished a good day's work he ambles out of town leisurely, carrying his empty baskets on a shoulder pole. On his way back there is a well every mile or so, the water is sweet and cool, and a drink of it drives the heat away. The pedlar thinks: there's no reason why people living on the main street should suffer so — crowding together under this heat, without even the shade of a tree where they can catch the breeze, and working strict hours whether the sun is high up in the sky or not. But the girls in town are really nice, with such fair complexions and soft skin; the men in town are fortunate indeed.

The townsfolk, on the other hand, pity the villagers who cannot even find a place to hide under the burning sun. Their shoulders and legs are covered in blisters, and their skin peels off layer after layer. The sun also makes the colour of their clothes fade and they never wear anything the least colourful. What a monotonous life! But the melons are really something. The inexplicable thing is why the couple at the middle school keep their door shut even in this burning weather. It would be understandable if it were only at night, but is it necessary to keep the door shut in the middle of the day too? Not unless they can't hold out until nightfall; imagine doing that when the sun is high, it must be excruciatingly hot! And yet though they are at it day and night, there is never any sign of them having a baby. The woman looks like an unmarried girl, her tummy flat, her waist and buttocks narrow, and her skin soft and supple.

Even after the hottest period is over and the calendar says that it is autumn, the heat lasts another eighteen days.

After these eighteen burning days, the theatrical troupe sends some of its members to a major company in a southern seaside city to learn new routines. Since only principal dancers and actors are allowed to go, the two of them are left behind, still practising every day, and still doing things the wrong way. She has grown even taller and bigger, and in comparison he, who has not grown at all, looks as though he has actually shrunk. She feels that she is becoming too big, that her body has become a burden. When she takes a wash and looks at her unusually full breasts, she is shocked and worried. She doesn't know why they have grown so big, and she doesn't know what will happen if they go on developing. She even suspects that this may be a strange illness. The thought makes her head swell, and she is so scared that she wants to cry. She studies every single part of her body, all so big, and she becomes afraid of herself. She knows that she is too big, but there is no way she can make herself smaller. In the company of the troupe's slim and refined girls she can't help feeling lowly and inferior because of her size. Besides, she never thinks before she speaks and so her words always seem incoherent or out of place. Her intelligent companions all call her Big Soppy. Fortunately she is someone who doesn't think much, so her feelings of inferiority and fear do not affect her health in the slightest. She is energetic, and her appetite is huge. At night when she climbs into bed, she hugs herself with her own arms, feeling extremely fond of herself. And then she falls soundly asleep, like a baby, without the least care in the world. In her sleep she frequently makes noises with her mouth, the sounds of a pampered child.

The burden for him is his maturity. At heart he seems a fully grown man, filled with shameless desire so mean and base that it frightens him. At first he did not know which part of his body was the seat of such desire; if he did, he would surely be determined to destroy that part of himself. And then one night he wakes up at an inappropriate time, and it suddenly dawns on him where his sin originates; to him it is all sin. But by this time he has realized how impossible it is to destroy that part of himself, and what's more, because it is such an important part he begins to treasure his desires as well. He does not understand why this is so.

And now the ones who had gone to learn new routines have come back, wearing stylish clothes and carrying the latest in travelling bags. They get off the ferry, step onto the unsteady gangway and make their way to the bank. Both of them have come to welcome the returning team. She has not succeeded in pushing her way to the front, and so has not been able to

lay her hands on a single bag, but she's excited and happy all
the same. She either walks in front of the group as if she is
clearing the way for an army, or walks at the back as though
to make sure that everything is all right, all the while
babbling about irrelevant things. No one answers her; no one
hears her. Yet if it were not for her and her prattle the
occasion would not have been so lively.

He walks in the centre of the group, next to the principal
dancer who always plays the male lead in dance dramas. The
principal dancer puts one arm round his shoulders. Though
he never attracts much attention he and the principal dancer
are the best of friends, and the latter confides in him. On the
way from the pier to the theatre, the principal dancer says to
him:

"You'll get a new role."

The role is the young Red Army soldier in the *pas de deux*
"Hard Times". It is impossible to find someone as small as
him and technically as brilliant. In other troupes this role is
always danced by a woman. The role seems custom-made for
him; it suits him so perfectly that no questions are raised and
he is cast for it. It is all smooth sailing except for one thing —
there are many lifts in the dance, and in one particular
section the old soldier is required to carry the young one on
his back while performing difficult steps, showing his
robustness and strength. At this point his major defect is
revealed. Though he looks small he is incredibly heavy. The
"old soldier" just does not have the strength to carry him; he
bends under his weight, unable to perform a single step.
Moreover, neither of them has had practice in lifts in *pas de
deux*, and as a result they do not know how to make the lifts
easier. He clings to his partner's back with all his might, and
though he feels embarrassed and apologetic it doesn't help.
When he clumsily jumps off his partner's back time and

again, his partner can't help complaining,

"You really are too heavy."

He turns red, countering, "You're just chicken!"

Anger darkens his partner's face, and a confrontation seems unavoidable. The principal tries to smooth things over, saying:

"I'll have a go."

The principal dancer walks through the steps carrying him on his back, but though he succeeds in doing this he can't catch his breath afterwards. Then all the others come up to him and take turns walking around carrying him on their backs, laughing. Finally he has had enough, and struggles to get back on the ground, giving the person under him a hard push. This at last puts an end to the joke on him.

In the evening he skips dinner, staying in the studio to improve his *baloné*. He knows that the initial jump is all-important; if he could get on to his partner's back with ease, what follows would be no problem at all. But if he exhausts himself trying to cling to his partner and fail to coordinate his breathing with the steps, there'll be trouble. Besides, he also wishes that he could take things more easily.

After a short while, she, too, comes to practise. She practises every day after dinner as if she thinks it's good for digestion. Thus she can eat more; she loves eating and has a great appetite. Today she is wearing a new, peach-coloured leotard, one of those the travellers have brought back with them for distribution to the troupe. This is one of the regular leotards used by the big companies, with a very low neckline, especially at the back where it reaches almost down to the waist. The elasticized welts around the legs are too tight, and cut deeply into her thighs.

All of a sudden he asks her amicably to help him rehearse the lifts in the dance. She has not heard him speak so mildly

to her for a long time, and besides, she has had a stupid urge
to show off since that afternoon, so she readily consents. First
of all he takes her through the paces; but that afternoon she
had stood on one side watching them rehearse and taken note
of every movement, so now she does every step correctly. He
then goes to the electrician for a tape-recorder and the music
tape, speedily locates that section of the music and starts the
tape. He climbs onto her back, and strangely, she doesn't feel
burdened at all. On the contrary, the exuberant music makes
her very happy. He performs his movements on her back,
feeling secure; he had not thought that her back would be so
broad, firm and strong. They go through the paces like a
dream, and at the end of it she's panting only a little, as is
normal. Before he speaks she says eagerly:

"Let's do it one more time!"

This time they take it from the top. She has learned all the
old soldier's steps and her rendering is not at all bad; she
actually expresses the heightened emotions rather well. When
it comes to the lift, he gets on to her back with perfect ease.
She has strong, powerful arms. Since she makes light of the
burden, his confidence increases and his movements become
bolder and more adroit, thus making it even easier for her.
Gradually they become familiar with the way each other
moves, and he finds that the understanding between them is
better than what he had achieved with his original partner.
After going through the dance five or six times, they become
at ease with the movements and dance without hesitation,
forgetting the technical difficulties and the need for mental
preparation before the lift. Every gesture of the arm and every
movement of the leg seem second nature to them. And the
music is uplifting; every repetition makes it more intimate
and more beautiful. She has forgotten that her role is that of
an old Red Army soldier, and thinks that she is just playing

herself; he has also forgotten that his role is a young soldier, and thinks that he is just playing himself. Every movement has become their own, an expression of their feelings and instincts. They have forgotten themselves in the dance; their images flash across one mirror onto another until they are surrounded by images of themselves. They actually feel that they are beautiful, and they never feel better about themselves than when they dance. Besides, there is also the music.

As he climbs on her back once again he smells the heavy odour of sweat; he feels the firmness of her back on his chest, exposed by the low-cut leotard, naked, warm and wet. His equally warm, wet chest rubs against her back, making a noise, and the friction hurts a little. He can feel the strong movements of her waist with his knees and her rounded muscular shoulders and thick neck with his hands. As she pants, her neck alternately tenses up and relaxes. Her hair, soaked in sweat, is plaited and fixed to the back of her head with hairpins. The tip of her plait brushes against his nose, and he can smell the strong odour of oil and sweat while a cool hairpin pricks his cheek. All his senses are aroused, freed from the dance techniques, and he tenses up once again. But this is a different kind of tension. Instead of suppressing all physical and emotional sensations, now every sense and every feeling is strained, fine-tuned and activated. Dancing has become for him just mechanical movements, unworthy of the slightest attention. He is carried on the back of a burning body; a burning body is moving energetically under him. Even the tiniest breath is communicated to his most sensitive nerve, igniting his hope which is erupting like lightning and fire.

The light and heat are passed on to her. She cannot feel anything besides the scorching brazier of red-hot coal on her back. The heat has become unbearable, and yet when he gets down and the burning sensation disappears, she feels an emptiness on her back and yearns for him to be up there again. When he gets back up on her back she feels that her heart and lungs are all on fire and wishes to roll on the ground to extinguish the flames scorching her body. But the music and the dance won't let her lie down. She seems to be controlled by a mighty and invisible will, repeating the routine over and over again, lifting him on to her back, then casting him to the ground. Suddenly she feels completely at ease; her panting stops and her breathing is synchronized with the tempo of her movements. Her body moves of its own accord.

The movements of their bodies are perfectly co-ordinated. He feels easy and confident jumping on to her back, never making the slightest mistake, as though that is the place where he truly belongs and the jumps which he performs on the ground are just expressions of his impatience to be up there again. Her mind is only at ease when he is on her back; the heavy burden pressed tightly against her gives her great pleasure. They seem glued together in all their movements, inseparable and intimate. He rolls on her back, jumping up and getting off, and the friction is dear to him, quenching the thirst of his flesh and soul. And the weight of his whole body, with all the rolling, jumping and rubbing is but a caress to her. His movements obviously hurt her; her back bends under the weight and her legs shake, but the dance goes on without a single missed step. The music is repeated continuously, interminably, and becomes more and more exuberant, never allowing a moment's rest.

It is now late into the night, and someone roars at the studio, cursing them for disturbing his sleep. Someone else opens and shuts a window with a loud bang. But they are oblivious to all these noises. The music envelops their world, an exuberant world totally out of control.

Finally someone turns off the electricity mains. The light suddenly goes off and the music stops; around them all is dark. The lights in the courtyard are turned off too, and there is no moon in the sky. It is pitch black, like the bottom of an abyss. He was on her back when their movements stopped with the music, frozen. Thirty seconds pass before he lands on the floor. Without uttering a single word, they run away in fear. The strange thing is they manage not to run into each other or fall down in this darkness, but just disappear like puffs of smoke.

In the end a girl is cast as the little red soldier in "Hard Times". That is because he became as heavy as lead, and has grown more ponderous and clumsy by the day so that no one can manage to dance under his weight. For some strange reason he has lost whatever adroitness he had, and no matter who carried him he could not relax. His tenseness and clumsiness make him even more of a burden to carry. He has lost the feeling of that nightmarish night when he danced on her back. He cannot establish that same kind of understanding and intimacy with anyone but her, and yet she avoids him when they see each other, and he is afraid of seeing her too. They dare not even practise together anymore. When she is in the studio, he stays away, and when he is there, she stays away. Gradually they have arrived at a new understanding, an understanding that they will not be in the same place. Yet how he yearns for her! And though she does not long for him as obviously as he does for her, she becomes agitated. She loses her temper easily, and will start a quarrel for no reason at all, at the end of which, even if she has the upper hand, she will still wail fiercely. It's only a small courtyard, and her uncontrollable wailing fills every corner. He hides in his room, listening to her wailing, and feels heart-broken and happy at the same time.

After the period of intense heat, autumn makes one feel particularly fresh and cool. There is a transparency in the sunlight, and the air looks newly cleansed. A ray of sunlight hangs on the top branch of a poplar. Even the villagers look much fairer than before. This autumn a kind of metallic grey jacket is in fashion. It has a western-style collar and a slightly gathered waistline. If someone walks down the street dressed in this outfit all the passers-by will stop to admire it. The first one to wear such a jacket is the foreign woman in the provincial middle school. She parades on the street, carrying a shopping basket to buy crabs from the "wild cat" who has come from the mouth of a certain River Mou. The locals call boat-people "wild cats", and pity these homeless and rootless drifters from the bottom of their hearts. The crabs, struggling fiercely with their claws all extended, are put into the woman's basket, their mouths foaming. They climb up the sides of the bamboo basket, but she shows no fear at all, picking them up one by one and putting them back into the basket. By mid-day everyone in the street is talking about it — that couple in the middle school, how can they eat something like that!

While this information is being circulated, the "wild cat" is back on his boat and rowing away. He thinks: what a ridiculous and noisy bunch of people, staying put in one place for generations on end, with no chance of seeing the world, as though they were rooted there! He looks at his wife seated in the stern nursing the baby, her eyes resting on the rippling green water, completely at ease. She keeps the lap of her garment in position with one hand, and manages to stroke the baby's face with a finger. Tall willow trees neatly line the bank, their branches bending low. The "wild cat" is content.

She is seventeen this autumn, he twenty-one. And they are still trying to avoid each other. The memory of that night is always on their mind; they simply cannot get away from it. They try to pretend that they have forgotten about it, or that they don't care, so that they can get along as normal. But as soon as they glance at each other, such pretence becomes ineffectual, and they hide away, not daring to see each other. Though they do not see each other, they are totally occupied with each other. His imagination runs riot. In his mind he has relived the experiences of that night thousands of times, and they have become so familiar to him that he begins to read endless meanings into them, so much so that he shocks himself. She is not an imaginative person, and has never been one to use her head. However, the experience of that night is frequently revived in her body, giving rise to an endless physical yearning. She does not know what she is yearning for, but feels that her body has been neglected, that she is surrounded by a desert of loneliness. She feels completely hollow. This nameless yearning torments her, and since she cannot find a way out she takes to gorging. She feels much better when she's eating, and so she eats a lot, never stopping until she is too full to take any more. At the same time she becomes lazy about practising. She gains weight rapidly; every part of her body tries its best to inflate itself, making her ugly and ungainly. He, on the other hand, is losing weight. You can see his bones sticking out of his skin, which is covered in scars because acne inflames his every pore. He looks exactly like a little chick with all its feathers plucked. Having lost his appetite, he tries to regain it by buying large portions of the best food served, which he takes to the studio, where he places it on the cement floor and sits himself on a ledge, staring at the food with hatred. He doesn't touch the food for a long time; he doesn't practise much either.

The studio looks forlorn.

The two of them look forlorn.

And then the troupe starts performing; the venue is the only theatre in town. This theatre looks like a huge warehouse, with its triangular roof supported by a thick unpainted beam onto which the stage lights are fixed. An unpainted pillar stands in the middle of the theatre, obstructing the view of the two seats right behind it. At every show the people seated here have to fight for a better view of the stage, but the seats are sold at the full price all the same because no one remembers their numbers. Cigarette butts and traces of phlegm stick to the cement floor, which is covered in a layer of dust and soil, never swept clean. The electricity supply is often cut, and when that happens the whole theatre becomes pitch black. There is a commotion, and then a gas lamp is lighted in front of the purplish-red velvet curtain, the light shining eerily on the worn-out velvet. Another lamp is lighted, then a third, a fourth, unfolding in a line along the curtain. The light shines from the ground upwards, illuminating the faces on stage and casting ugly shadows on them.

But this has nothing to do with them. They are back-stage, she taking care of the costumes, he of the props, and when there is nothing to do they watch the performance from the wings where the set pieces are lined up. They are separated by a few layers of curtains and set pieces, she standing in the shadow of one set piece and he another, only a couple of paces from each other. But against the brilliance of the stage the wings look even dimmer, and they do not see each other. They watch the items on the programme being performed one by one. At last it comes to the dance "Hard Times". The music starts suddenly; the music they know so well that it sounds almost unfamiliar to them now. At that same moment both

of them shiver, and the shivers are like two currents of electricity meeting up in mid-air, establishing a link, so that each
becomes aware of the other's presence nearby. They nevertheless remain where they are, their hearts thumping. He turns
to look, and his eyes look straight into hers. Suddenly she takes
a step backwards, disappearing into the shadow of a huge set
piece depicting a military camp. He too steps back at once,
in pursuit. Behind the set piece it is pitch black. From the
stage the music soars, filling the whole theatre and envelop-
ing everything. He stands there for a while, then stretches his
hands out, groping; he doesn't touch anything, but feels that
she is trying to avoid him. Her clumsy movement has disturbed
the calm air currents, and he hears the sound very clearly, a
sound so loud that it is like waves and bores. Then he steps
forward a little and grabs her hand, which she still tries to pull
away, but he holds on tightly and twists it. She seems to let
out an "ouch!" and then her back is pressed against his chest.
He forcefully twists her shoulders and turns her around; she
can't help but lean against him. He is so strong that no one
would ever be able to struggle free. With his other hand he
forces her to turn her head around and face him. His lips find
hers, biting almost viciously, and she ceases to struggle. The
music is approaching the end, with the horns, drums and all
the other instruments joining in. Seething and swelling, its
strength would shake whole nations, and all small and hum-
ble noises are drowned in it.

It is as though a river, long frozen, has melted, and spring
waters pour down-stream. Nobody understands why all of a
sudden they look blooming. She is so pretty that people can
forgive her for her clumsy and gigantic body. Her eyes have
never shone as brightly, her lips have never been as moist and
her complexion never as clear as they now appear. Her hair
is black and thick, and her skin, slightly dark, is as soft and

smooth as satin. Her proportions are still not right, but the outline of the parts which are out of proportion has softened and is thus less irritating to the eye. Moreover, her facial expression has obviously changed. She seems more confident now, always wearing a self-congratulatory smile on her face. Though she looks a little stupid, the sense of joy and openness is still most appealing.

As for him, the acne on his face and his body has subsided, and the brown scars have become lighter in colour. The sticky, yellowish mixture of oil and sweat no longer comes out of his pores, and his face looks much cleaner. As a result one begins to notice his rather handsome features. With his straight noise, prominent eyebrows and deep-set eyes, he looks like an Albanian. Well, these days Albanian films are the only Western films you can see, and gradually a set of asethetic standards have evolved around the characters appearing in these films. His eyes have a natural lustre, giving the impression that he is always deep in thought. This makes him look serious, even profound, and not at all supercilious. Thus, even with a body like a fifteen-year-old's, he still gives the impression that he is a man.

It seems that the obstacles in their way have been washed away, and their lives can flow unhindered, leaping and dancing with vitality. They are no longer afraid of each other, and only avoid each other in the presence of the others, thus giving this exercise an additional sense of fun and mystery, as though they have the laugh on all humanity. Like enemies they ignore each other as they brush past one another, their eyes looking straight ahead, but in their hearts they exchange mysterious glances and cunning smiles, feeling ever so proud of themselves. When no one else is around, they are inseparable, as if glued together. They don't really know what love is; they only know that they cannot suppress their need for each other.

Every day at nightfall the two of them disappear, leaving the dark studio behind. Then as the polar star sinks in the west and morning mist whitens the pitch black night , they appear in the courtyard, one after the other, like ghosts, their hair tousled, their clothes untidy and their eyes shining in the dark. Treading on the wet stone slabs they steal back into their dormitories. It has been a night of bliss. After the excitment of petting and rubbing against each other's body they feel blissfully exhausted and proudly languid. Their lover's touch seems to have seeped into their pores and mixed with their blood, which flows along their veins singing a happy tune. This feeling of blissfulness almost makes them sigh. They would like to tell everyone, to make everyone envious. But they must lock their bliss in their hearts, not allowing the smallest trace to leak out, because this is a sin. Although she is an ignorant girl she knows that she has transgressed. She does not know what is right, but she knows very well what is wrong. And he, who knows everything, understands perfectly that this is an unforgivable crime. Yet it gives so much enjoyment that it is irresistable. When their bodies touch and they become one, all these ideas of crime, sin, right and wrong no longer exist; there is only joy — the joy of excitment, of pain, and of fear.

Their initial response was fear, and it was also the first emotion they overcame. She, being unintelligent, can easily dissipate her fear, and he, being highly intelligent, knows how to control it. But now that they are no longer fearful they actually regret it; they feel sad that their fear is no more. Both the unintelligent girl and the intelligent boy will always remember the pleasure they had as they made love, trembling with fear. Fear had put up a stubborn resistance as desire launched a similarly stubborn attack, and in the fierce battle their bodies had experienced a strange and overwhelming sense of pleasure.

They are so close and loving to each other's body that it is impossible to deepen this love anymore, and so their souls declare open alliance. All of a sudden they are intimate and inseparable even in front of other people, and no one was prepared for this. They are practising together again, helping and taking care of each other. Even harsh words are meant to convey intimacy. They group their meal tickets together to buy their meals, which they share. She washes all his clothes, while he takes over her share of work on the stage, mounting and dismantling the scenes. She is not any weaker than he, but he will not let her do it, so she just hangs around eating carrots with green skin. If someone remonstrates with her she doesn't hesitate to answer back, and if she loses in the verbal contest he always comes to her aid. Such a strong alliance almost ensures that they will never meet with defeat.

But as the union of body and soul is still inadequate to give vent to the intensity of their love, they begin to vent their feelings via a diametrically opposite channel — that of animosity. Just as they flaunted their intimacy in front of everyone, so their open rows have become the subject of much public contempt. For a period of time they really become enemies. When they are alone with each other, their physical attraction stems from a strong sense of repulsion. They try to resist one another as though in mortal combat, both unwilling to give in, wringing and pulling at each other's body until they are both exhausted. And then, all tenderness, they love each other. Yet after the act of love the combat is resumed.

In the presence of others they look at each other with enmity in their eyes and speak with a venomous tongue. They can't come up with a single decent word, but keep swearing at each other in the filthiest language. The others threaten to report them to the director of the troupe so that they will be punished, but always to no avail. Thus they go on, blowing hot and cold unpredictably, as though they had been indebted to each other in their previous lives and there is no settling of this debt.

This is a troublesome autumn.

It rains continuously for days, and the river is lost behind the drizzle and the mist. Like a wandering spirit, the ferry drifts in a stretch of mist and water, docking at the pier, then floating away. The earthen paths out of town are all swamped, ruined by trampling feet. The villagers walking barefoot into town spread the mud and filthy water all over the streets. Even leeches have found their way onto the streets, and someone actually dsicovered a leech which is only found in southern China. Everyone in town panics. Though they all know that the production company in the suburb has recently turned some of their fields into rice paddies, and that the leech must have come from there, they still can't get rid of this sense of ill omen. The leech is extremely dexterous. Once it bites into your leg it never lets go, and when you forcibly brush it away there appears on your leg a bottomless pit. It is only after a while that the blood starts to drip.

The rain gradually stops and the ground gradually dries up; but then the weather turns cold all of a sudden, and it is winter.

Just as the summer was extraordinarily hot, so this winter is uncommonly cold. There is no wind, and the sun shines cheerfully as on a mild spring day, but the cold is like a knife, cutting into your hands, your feet and your face. Your nose and ears are as red as radishes. Even if you stand in the sun in the middle of the street you won't be able to hold out for more than thirty seconds. The cold is biting, yet shows no obvious sign of its severity. A sense of uneasiness drifts through the streets like a wandering spirit, as if something extraordinary is going to happen.

And sure enough, just after Chinese New Year the news comes that Premier Zhou Enlai has passed away.

Since the sense of uncertainty has been given a concrete answer, the uneasiness gradually subsides.

And then General Zhu De, Commander-in-Chief of the People's Liberation Army, also passes away;

And then comes the earthquake in Tangshan;

And then the country's leader Chairman Mao passes away;

And then,

Comes the fall of the Gang of Four.

It is another autumn, and they have grown a year older; she is now eighteen and he twenty-two. But they feel that they are a hundred years older, and what took place the previous autumn seems to have happened in their previous lives.

They have tried to love too hard and too abundantly, they have known no restraint. As a result they are spent both physically and emotionally, and now they actually feel tired. To ward off this feeling they put greater effort and fervour into their love. But their bodies have gone through such intense and varied exercise that they have become a little numb, and new stimuli are needed to arouse their response and vitality. They exhaust their imagination trying to find new ways and positions, but familiarity has eroded the sense of mystery and fun. Yet they cannot stop either; neither can do without the other. Although they come back exhausted, annoyed and disappointed every time, they still look forward to each outing with fervent expectation.

They come back pouring with sweat and climb up the narrow wooden staircase, which creaks underneath their weight; the sound seems to tickle the soles of their feet. They feel both tired and dirty, but they don't feel like going for a wash. The

stove has been extinguished, and as they had gone out in a
hurry they had forgotten to put hot water into their own flasks.
Now their flasks are empty, and they dare not use the water
in other people's flasks for fear that this would betray
something. All is quiet in the courtyard. They lie in bed
thoroughly exhausted, feeling extremely uncomfortable from
the stickiness of their bodies. Even the quilts are wet. They
simply cannot understand why it is that, with so much effort,
the ecstacy of the early days still eludes them. At the same
time they cannot help being ashamed of themselves; they long
to be reborn, to live a new life, and they swear their determination to themselves. But come the next day, when they
see each other, they make the same old sign and give each
other the same meaningful look, thus confirming again their
next rendezvous. They are as agitated as ants on a hot stove
in the few hours before the meeting, but fortunately by now
their endurance is well trained, and no one ever notices
anything wrong from their behaviour. They pass the few hours
of waiting, their agitation unnoticed by anyone, and then they
sneak out of the courtyard.

They fling themselves into each other's arms feverishly, and
yet in the split second when they touch, they turn cold. All
the sensations are now familiar to them; there is not the least
novelty or curiosity, not even fear or pain. They go through
it like some insignificant interlude on stage, feeling nothing
but depressed. There is no joy in it; they have only made
themselves filthy and they will never become innocent again.
Only now do they feel sad and remorseful, but it is too late.

In the troupe more and more members are falling in love.
It seems that the whole troupe has paired off, and the lovers
do everything together. The two of them should really have
joined this "lovers' squad", indeed they should have become
its leaders, but they are weighed down by shame and feel that

they do not qualify. Everyone else seems so innocent compared
with them; everyone has a bright future. But they have fallen
into the mire, and can never wash themselves clean. So it is
that at a time when falling in love has become the vogue, they
hide their feelings and treat each other as strangers. The others
all think that they are again fighting over something, and since
this is nothing new, they are left to sort it out between
themselves. No one understands their misery. Since both of
them are plagued by the same misery, they each have their
own share, and there is little they can do in the way of shar-
ing the burden or counselling each other. Together they take
up the burden, but there is no communication, no mutual
consolation. In fact they understand each other thoroughly,
but the least hint of understanding brings embarrassment and
worry, and they can see absolutely no way out. They are
therefore extremely lonely in their despair. Each of them
shoulders his or her own share of despair, feeling that everyone
in the world is happier than they. They have been too rash,
too impatient and too extravagant in their search for happiness,
so that by now it is all used up, leaving only shame and despair.

Since they are in despair and must shoulder their own share
of its burden without help, they begin to hate each other. This
is serious, earnest hatred, so serious that they no longer fight
in front of others because they feel that it would be too
frivolous and pretentious. They fight only when no one is
around and they are ferocious when they quarrel, each aim-
ing the vilest words at the other's weakest spot. She screams
at him in tears: "I hate you. I'll kill you!" He grasps her throat
with both hands and threatens in a strangled voice: "Scream
again, and I'll throttle you." She really hates him, and he really
wants to throttle her, thus they become fearful, and their hands
become weak. Their agitation is real, and as they berate each
other their anger mounts, and they start hitting and beating

each other, their bodies entangled. While his physical strength seems enormous, her spirit is so roused that she can stand up to anything. At the end of this contest their anger gradually subsides, but their feelings are still excited. They cannot tell whether they are hitting or caressing each other, or maybe they are hitting and caressing at the same time. At this moment it seems that earth and sky and everything else have vanished, only an indescribable feverish urge remains. From deep inside their bodies a strange sense of joy rises; the joy that has been lost to them, that they have yearned for and waited for in desperation, comes back to them unexpectedly, at a time when they are totally unprepared.

At last they are exhausted from the physical contest, and lie down completely limp. But they have not felt such a deep sense of satisfaction for a long time. Gradually they quieten down and take a look at each other; there is no hatred in that look, only love and intimacy. They then hold each other by the hand and, as innocent as two school children going home on vacation, walk on, gently swinging their hands. The mere touch of their hands makes them feel intimate, and they only let go when they are within a hundred metres of the courtyard. Then they feel again their suppressed sense of inferiority.

The sound of singing and musical accompaniment come from the courtyard, but it seems to come from a different world. Again they feel physically filthy, like two wild dogs which have just climbed out of the mire. They have completely lost their dignity in front of each other; they are like two books in each of which the ugly history of the other is recorded. They wish that the other would go to a far away place, or even leave this world, taking their shame away so that they could make a new beginning and live a clean life again. The sense of hatred grows once more, never to be extinguished.

On the main road beneath the flood-gate a tractor keeps

coming and going noisily, and people keep seeing a man-ghost
fighting with a woman-ghost. The woman-ghost's hair is in
disarray, and the man-ghost swears with a mouth all bloody;
they make creaky noises as they fight. The story travels a long
way along the main road, gaining in colour and detail as it
goes, so that when it reaches the small town again it has taken
on a completely different look. On a comparatively quiet and
peaceful night the two of them sit listening to the story with
others, fearful at heart.

They want to be rid of each other. He begins to be cold
towards her, and then she becomes cold too. They don't feel
sad because of this coldness, on the contrary they are relieved, it is like taking a rest after a fierce battle. His life resumes
its previous tempo — daily practice, then a wash, dinner and
bed. He doesn't sleep too badly either, and as a result becomes
more light-hearted and even-tempered.

But after such an experience they both look old, much older
than their real age. She actually loses weight, and her skin sags,
leaving her thighs all crinkled with ripples. He, on the other
hand, gains weight. In their hearts they feel old. To them,
the love affairs of the young men and women in the troupe
are just childish games. They have seen through the curtains;
they have seen the truth.

She has become quite shameless, often forgetting that she
is still an unmarried girl, and that as a rule there are things
which she is not supposed to talk about or listen to. She doesn't
care at all, it all seems so natural to her; even going into the
gent's by mistake does not bother her. She cannot understand why the others make fun of her, and she is hurt and baffl-
ed. As for him, the unspoken rules governing male-female
relationships have long been torn to shreds. In his eyes all
women are naked; he can see their most private parts at a
glance. It is impossible for him to keep the distance between

himself and women, a distance which is necessary if he is to
experience pure and sacred sentiments for the other sex. This
leaves him in great pain. The world has disclosed to him all
its secrets at such an early stage, what more is there to arouse
his curiosity and interest? For him life is all gloom and
despondency; it seems that he has barely begun to live when
life comes to a dead end for him. It is only now that they realize
however cold they are to each other, and even though they
are no longer together, they have sinned, and will remain sin-
ners. They are unclean; at such a young age they are already
unclean. How long will they have to live in such uncleanliness?
So, when they are apart, they become soul mates.

*expect society*

And yet they do not have the courage to be together again.
Each is afraid; afraid of what the consequences might be if
they carry on as before. But even at their most determined
moments, deep in their hearts neither of them really believes
that this is the end of their relationship. They are just waiting;
waiting for the day when they can wait no longer, and then
they will see what happens. They live their lives as before, returning to the dormitory early every night, and going straight
to bed, thinking that they are at peace with themselves and
happy. But they are only living out a self-allotted period of
restraint. They both sense that this is not really the end,
because unbeknown to them, neither of them wants it to end
just like this. However, the sense of peace and relief is not
unreal either. They had really been too excited, too tired, and
needed a good rest to recuperate.

A sin like theirs is like a seed. Once it has reached the soil
there is little hope that it will just die. They live in a time
of bleak ignorance; there is no forerunner to help them see
the light. Besides, there are some things in which even the
sages would not have been able to help. We can only grope,
search, crawl and scramble in the dark, trying to find a way

out of the filth and mire. Adam and Eve are our examples. After they had eaten the forbidden fruit even God was unable to save them, but had to cast them out of Eden and condemn their descendents to endless suffering. The two of them are just children, simple and lowly. How can we expect them to conquer the forces of nature? All they can fall back on are their innate inclination towards good or evil, and their intelligence, and so they are alternately dominated by the forces of darkness and the forces of light.

In this manner spring passed peacefully.

They seem to have reached their ultimate destiny and have settled down in peace. They are not on particularly good terms, nor do they quarrel; theirs has become an ordinary relationship. Sometimes they chat about unimportant things, sometimes they practise together, but the practice is never of much use. Even the gossip about them has died down, and when people really have too much time on their hands and talk about the two of them again, it is treated as something past. Even they themselves think that it is all past, that their fervent lust has passed rapidly like a hurricane, and the danger is now lifted. Gradually they have relaxed, and are no longer as mentally alert as before. It even gets to the point where their relationship seems to have returned to its earliest stage. She will yell and scream at him, heedless of anything, and he bears with her forgivingly. It is as if nothing has ever happened between them. Even when they are alone together they can be at peace now. Sometimes they actually wonder whether they have really had that kind of relationship. They can recall every occasion, every detail with such vividness, and yet it all seems like a dream.

In fact they are both at a stage of rest and recovery. Though they have left their feelings of exhaustion and tension behind, they have not yet recovered their vital energy, and they are still physically weak. It is as if they are slightly intoxicated, so drowsy and somnolent are they, as if they have not fully awoken from their sleep. It is indeed a blissful time, but it will not last, it will in fact be gone in a split second. In its wake will come an earth-shaking storm, so horrendous that in comparison what happened to them before was but lightning arching across the sky before a storm, or the sound of thunder roaring from afar; it was only a prelude, an introduction, a prophecy. Since they are weak and fearful, what happened has almost frightened them out of their wits, almost broken their nerve. Fortunately they are young, healthy and simple-minded, and have a fair share of curiosity, so they have actually recovered rather speedily, and now await the formal, torrential baptism of life.

They have resumed their daily practice and seem to be reliving the good old days. They stretch and contract their bodies in defiance of natural law, panting with joy and relief after the tremendous pain and exhaustion. They feel their sweat pouring out, washing away all the dirt and filth inside them, and then they wash down after sweating, the scalding water running down their bodies and pricking them like needles. The joy of practice that they had forgotten so long ago is once more aroused. She feels as light as a feather, pirouetting hundreds of times nonstop, until her strength is gone and she collapses on the floor. The triangular ceiling of the studio keeps on revolving rhythmically; she actually feels that she is still pirouetting, that she will go on like this forever. She feels that her body is healthy, strong, and obedient to her wishes, that she can perform any step with ease. It is impossible that she would forget any step; she knows them too well. But since she has not practised for a long time they have now become new to her, new and yet familiar. The image of her pirouetting is reflected a dozen times in the studio mirrors and she sees dozens of her duplicates pirouetting on all sides, as if she has multiplied dozens of times and every self is dancing, or every self is watching her in admiration. She is enthralled.

His body displays a suppleness and strength hitherto unknown to him. He stands erect, gazing quietly in front of him, and then bends backwards very, very slowly. His head is upside down, and the world is reversed in his calm gaze. Then he raises his hands until they are level with his shoulders, and just as his head is going to touch the ground, his hands meet the floor, and he moves them forward very gradually until they touch his heels. Now he raises his head again, and everything that had been reversed is now returned to normal under his gaze. He watches calmly, feeling no strain and no pain. This posture seems natural to him, a normal way of standing. As he gazes, she flashes into sight like a whirlwind, then flashes out of sight again. Something seems to be flowing smoothly along her whirlpool-like pirouettes, and along the tracks of his bent body. They both seem to feel the currents of this underground river and to hear the sound of its waters.

The time has come for the troupe to go and perform in the south.

On the day the troupe leaves town, every family along the main street is steaming glutinous rice dumplings for the dragon-boat festival.[1] The whole street is filled with the fresh fragrance of the bamboo leaves used for making the dumplings. At the break of dawn the ferry slowly makes its way towards the pier, and as it pulls up people suddenly rush out like a flood, tramping down the gangway to shore, their shoulder poles hitting against each other. Members of the

---

[1] The fifth day of the fifth month according to the Lunar calendar. A festival which commemorates the death of the poet Qu Yuan (fl. 340 B.C. — 278 B.C.), who threw himself into a lake after he lost favour with the prince.

troupe have to wait for everyone to disembark before they board the ship, carrying boxes of props, costumes, lighting, painted scenes and stage wings. After everything has finally been put on board and everyone has embarked, the ferry sets out again. The sun has risen, and is hidden behind the lush willows on the far bank, seemingly bashful. The water-men's songs flow on the golden river, their voices sometimes resonant, sometimes low, accompanied by the sound of rolling cart wheels. As the morning mist disperses, the songs suddenly become loud and clear, but also indescribably desolate, leaping from the water and rising ever higher into the sky. The cart wheels roll from one muddy track to another, jolting the cart with every change of track, spilling a little water from the tanks, and at that point the song quivers. The water-men's songs are thus forever marked with pauses and quivering notes, a record of the road's roughness.

The sun rises higher and higher.

The ferry travels slowly against the current, and the sun follows, travelling along the corridor of willows. Ripples in the river shine like scales, and a current of clear water rolls beneath the ferry, mixing with a current of muddy water. The cabin is damp, as if it has just been washed, but it is dirty, as if it has never been washed. Cigarette butts, phlegm, melon seeds and chicken droppings cover the floor. People squeeze themselves onto the half-rotted benches, their ears so filled with the noise of the engine that they can hear nothing else.

The two of them sit in the lower cabin, and whether intentionally or not, they are actually sitting next to each other. The lower cabin is particularly stuffy and damp. From a row of windows you can see the legs of those who are standing by the railings on deck. It looks as if they are standing and walking on the shoulders of those in the cabin. At times these legs crowd together, and at times they part, so sunlight

is occasionally let into the cabin, and at other times blocked.
But in either case the cabin is always dark. There is an electric
light bulb covered in a layer of dust and enveloped in smoke.
The smoke is from the cheap tobacco leaves which you push
into long pipes and then inhale deeply; you then exhale
clouds of smoke so strong that it makes you cough. If you keep
smoking for any length of time you will be a little dizzy. The
ferry rocks slightly, and the dim light bulb wavers with it. The
smoke in the cabin also wavers, and human feet walk on
human shoulders, it is all like a dream. Everyone is drowsy.
People sitting on the benches squeeze against each other,
shoulder crushing against shoulder, so that they have to hunch
over. There is also very little space between the facing benches, and people sit knee pushing against knee. Nothing is
more difficult than to walk between these two rows. Passengers
try to get some sleep, pressing their foreheads against their
knees. Their heads rock on their knees, hitting against one
knee then the other.

The two of them are squeezed against one another, shoulder
pressing against shoulder, leg against leg. She lays her head
on the bag she placed on her own knees, and has nearly fallen
asleep. He looks out of the window, through the chinks between human legs, at the misty stretch of water and sky, and
has nearly fallen asleep too. The roar of the engine fills your
head; the whole world seems to have sunk deep inside its din.
The smoke of cheap tobacco gradually loses its bitter taste,
and becomes quite sweet, but it is a sickly sweetness which
paralyzes your senses. They are almost asleep; only a thread
of their consciousness remains awake, floating like a thread
of silk in the air. This thread of consciousness winds round
their totally relaxed and unalert bodies, tickling them. It is
like a worm caressing the arm of a child lying on a cool, green
lawn under the warm sun, fast asleep; it is like the feeling

of a mother's milk jetting against the tender throat of a baby; it is like spring rain, imperceptibly moistening the dried and cracked land; it is like a breeze that filters through the leaves on a stifling hot night, and brushes against your sweating body. The more soundly they sleep, the more active and daring this thread of consciousness becomes, probing deep into the most sensitive, hidden parts of their bodies. Finally it has spread all over their bodies, touching and caressing every part of them. They experience a sense of pleasure hitherto unknown to them, and sleep as if they were intoxicated, even snoring lightly. The thread of consciousness seems to consider its task accomplished; it too has become tired and gradually curbs its movements; it rests, then falls asleep.

At this moment they seem to be pushed by some kind of force, and the shock wakes them. Their hearts are beating fast, swinging like a pendulum, and their blood races through every vessel in their bodies, boiling. They feel that something in them has been awakened; it is now alive, and moving. Yes, something is awake, alive, moving. They dare not move; they dare not look at each other. Their shoulders and legs, pressed against each other, are now completely rigid, incapable of movement. Since their bodies are pressed tightly against each other on one side, they feel burning hot one moment, and icy cold the next. They blush, each hoping to get out of this situation, but each is irresolute, so they remain seated there, dazed.

The windows in the front suddenly brighten; nothing obstructs the view now. In front of them is a white stretch of water. It seems that the ferry is travelling along a corridor under the river, that they are travelling along a corridor under the river. They are so tightly squeezed against each other that it is impossible to move, as if they are tied together. Indeed an unseen rope seems to have tied them up from head to toe, so tightly that they will never be able to struggle free.

The sun has set long ago. It sank in a far off place in the direction of the bow. People are now tired of smoking, but the tobacco smoke seems to have congealed in the air. It hangs overhead, refuses to dissipate, and creates a sense of oppression. They feel stiff in the neck, as if grinding stones have been placed on their heads. A stomach rumbles; they cannot tell whether it is him or her; it is so loud that it almost drowns out the roar of the engine. They are hungry now. They fell asleep when meal was served and their friends did not wake them, so they missed it. Fortunately the ferry is now docking at the pier.

On this day, all the children in the city are wearing colourful string-nets around their necks, with a duck's egg inside each net; colourful tassels dance and sway at the bottom of the net; dancing and swinging in time with the egg. The train roars along the middle of the road, shaking the whole road. Every nostril is as black as a chimney. There are numerous multi-storied buildings of varying heights, standing square and squat, like match-boxes, looking arrogant and dumb at the same time. At night, bright little squares of windows shine on all four sides of the buildings. The street lamps, shaped like magnolias, hide behind the branches of scholartrees, and at regular intervals one lamp reveals its brightness, then another .... Cars speed past, heading in opposite directions, and tidal waves of bicycles flank the cars on both sides, clearing the way for them. The ringing of bicycle bells fill the air. The display windows of the stores are illuminated by fluorescent lights and reveal a host of brilliant colours. The walls next to the display windows are pasted with layers of posters; passers-by can see them thanks to the light from the displays. The posters announce a variety of provincial and regional plays given by troupes from all over the country; it is indeed a scene of festive prosperity.

The posters of their troupe are too small, only half the size of other posters, and are easily torn by the wind. The troupe dares not paste its posters on top of existing ones, and instead they are tucked alongside, like a small child hanging onto its granny. Yet the first three shows still boast a full house; there are so many people in this place! Of people, this city has more than its share. They push and squeeze against each other, and walk briskly and self-assuredly between cars speeding past. Car horns are tooted, so sharp and ear-piercng that the noise shakes the sky. Then all of a sudden a loud whistle comes from nowhere, and the car horns are silenced. A train roars past. The car horns resume their performance afterwards, but it has become just a little stealthy. If you look beyond the bright square blocks of buildings, you will see a pillar of dark smoke gradually rising against the deep blue sky, floating gracefully, and spreading itself into a beautiful black peony in full bloom. If you let your eyes wander, you will see that the whole sky is decorated with such beautiful black patterns, all constantly changing, creating a circle of fairy tales. The black smoke dissolves into the deep blue atmosphere, gradually darkening the sky. As a result, the lights shine ever more brightly against the black night.

Every day seven or eight ferries dock at the pier and then leave again, blowing sirens one after another.

Half of the people in the city are only travellers. They come by river and leave by road, or they come by road and leave by river.

Thus the city is particularly unquiet.

The troupe has rented a small theatre with only eight hundred seats. But it has a grand name — The People's Theatre. There is no dormitory attached, and the theatre people recommended a hostel nearby to the troupe. The bill per person per day would have taken up all the money they earn from their performances, so they have had to decline and fend for themselves. The projection room is turned into a dormitory for women. It is just a narrow corridor with a few holes in the wall as windows for the projectors. The noise, the heat and the smell of human bodies waft through these windows from the theatre, and make it even more stifling. There is only one big, long bench for everyone to squeeze on to and sleep on at night, like a kang in northeastern China. No one can really sleep the first night; they are itchy all over. Struggling to open their sleepy eyes, they turn on the light to discover that lice the size of small beans are crawling all over the straw mattresses.

The men have to sleep wherever they can, and with the audience gone, they can actually make a bed anywhere in the theatre. Married men find it difficult to adjust to this first night away from their wives; they toss and turn, and try to raise their spirits with the aid of memory and imagination. In the silence of the theatre voices reverberate loudly, and it is always dirty jokes; every single word travels to the projection room through the windows. The women pretend not to have heard, but they find it difficult to suppress their urge to laugh. They try hard, and they dare not look into each other's eyes for even the exchange of a single glance would lift the curtain between them. It is a night of unrest. The next morning everyone wakes up with red and puffy eyes, and a sallow, dirty-looking complexion.

The show goes on as usual.

They play to a highly critical audience here. The tiniest mistake brings an immediate reaction, often accompanied by rude abuse. As a result they have to be especially careful and attentive during the performance, suppressing their feelings of tiredness and heightening their spirits. But having worked themselves up, now they still feel excited though the performance is over, and since they have just had a snack, they do not feel sleepy at all though it is almost midnight. The weather is hot and suffocating, so they scatter about the theatre in groups of two or three, chatting and swapping stories. Some even go out of the theatre to catch the breeze in the streets. At first they just wander near the theatre door, but gradually they walk on, until they reach the river bank.

It is quiet here at night. The river is flowing slowly, gently lapping against the bank. A few lights glimmer in the cool, damp breeze. At first they walk in a group, then they pair off in silence and disappear one pair after another. The river bank is long anyway, and dark.

So it is that the two of them are again on their own. At first they were simply lagging behind the group; he didn't seem to have noticed her lagging behind, nor she him. They walk on on their own. There is no moon in the sky, and no stars. It is dark, and they are enveloped in the darkness, each wrapped in a curtain of night, walking on in solitude. In fact they are only a dozen paces from each other; he is walking among the willows right by the river, and she among the willows further from the bank. The earth underfoot is wet with dew, soft yet firm. They tread on it noiselessly. She stretches her arms to touch the willows on either side of her. She holds onto a willow tree on her left, and when her right hand touches another one, she lets go with her left hand to search for the one further in front, and thus she moves on. The tough tree bark scratches her palms; it hurts a little, but it is a pleasant feeling, a kindly pain, like Granny holding her by the hand. She feels naughty, and deliberately rubs her palms against the tree bark until they hurt.

He tears a willow branch off and winds it around his neck; it feels cool. He ties the willow branch into a noose and carefully tightens the noose from both ends. The cool willow branch sinks deeper and deeper into his neck, and with it the feeling of coolness. He is suffocating, but he feels happy. If the willow branch had not broken he would have tightened the noose further. He tears off another branch and repeats the game. In no time at all, broken and unbroken willow branches are hanging all over his body, turning him into a tree spirit.

The people in front have walked further and further away, but their jokes and laughter can still be heard very clearly. There is also the singing, rather out of tune. Now all of a sudden a star appears in the sky; minute and far away, but very bright. The darkness fades, and he sees the lively movements of someone on the other side of the willow trees. She also sees the strange figure hung with willow branches on the other side of the trees. They are not sure, but their heartbeats quicken. Another star lights up in the sky, a bigger one, and closer too; it looks as though it is going to fall ito the river. The darkness fades further, revealing a stretch of white mist. In the mist he sees her, and she him. Neither has turned round, but they have seen each other. She is still touching the willow trees alternately with her hands. The earth becomes softer and softer, and each time her foot leaves the ground it tries to hold her back with the utmost tenderness. The trees are becoming ever kindlier, as if they are kissing her palms with the purity of all their roughness. He keeps on tearing willow branches, making nooses and strangling himself. The cool sense of suffocation brings him increasing pleasure, and he has not noticed that a weal has appeared on his neck. He just feels relaxed and happy, so he says, as if to himself:

"What a fine day!"

An unexpected answer comes from the other side:

"Yes, indeed."

So he follows with this:

"The stars have come out."

And the other side answers:
"Yes, indeed."
Then he says:
"The moon is going to come out too."
The other side answers:
"Yes, indeed."
Her voice is still echoing in the air when a half moon comes
out, brightening earth and sky. Somehow the mist seems
thicker. Slowly he walks out from under the willow trees, and
slowly she walks out from under the willow trees; they both
approach the path in the middle. It is an earthern track covered
with some sand, which is now glittering in the moonlight.
"It's been really hot these few days,"he says to her. By now
they are standing shoulder to shoulder.
"I don't mind the heat," she says. Her hands are moist
and sticky, as if wet from the tears of the willows. She draws
her hands together and rubs them forcefully, producing a
screeching noise. He beats her hands with a willow branch:
"Stop rubbing; what do you think you're doing!"
The touch of the cool willow branch on her burning hot
hands brings no pain. Nevertheless she cowers to one side,
saying, "I want to!"
He beats her again with the willow branch. She dodges left
and right, and his willow branch follows her. She starts to run
away, and he goes in pursuit. She stretches her thick, long
legs, running like a deer chased by a wolf, her heart beating
fast. The tension is great, but so is her joy, and she starts gig-
gling. He runs with his waist bent, like a hare, almost boun-
ding along at ground level. He is agitated and excited, shivering slightly, so he clenches his teeth and makes absolutely no
sound. There is but the distance of a stride between them;
he stretches his arm and almost touches her. But she avoids
it. The laughter and songs in front now sound close-by, and

they can see a vague outline of their group. She cannot but slow down, and he grabs her. It seems that from very, very far downstream, a water-man's sorrowful song is travelling up against the current. But when you try to listen, it is drowned in the whistling wind.

The half moon disappears, and the stars dim. The mist is even thicker now; you cannot see beyond five paces. The singing voices in front have climbed up the embankment and left the river, but the songs linger as they gradually recede in the distance. The dark waters flow on, with an occasional glimmer of lamp-light.

Excited and exhausted, they walk hand in hand on their way back. Slowly they have come back into the city. The lights are still bright, and the trains still roar past. The clamour of human voices at the stations and the pier fill the whole city, so that even the night enjoys no peace or quiet. They walk on the narrow streets, and the hard cement road no longer absorbs their footsteps, which are clear and distinct as their shoes strike the ground. However carefully or softly they tread, the sound is still clear, musical. At the far edge of the sky there is a dim light, and they think it is dawn. They panic, feeling that they have done something unpardonable, and walk on briskly, no longer holding hands. "Too late!" they both think. They feel that everything is lurking in the darkness, watching them. "I'll never do it again," they both think, feeling that they have sinned, and run into the theatre.

The dim light at the edge of the sky is only lamplight which shines throughout the night. Nights in this city are always lit like that.

The theatre is pitch black; all the lights have been turned off. She gropes in the dark, finding her way up to the projection room. Finally she reaches the bed, and crawls onto it. Fearful that she will wake someone, she dares not take her clothes off, but goes to sleep just as she is. He is still groping by the side of the pitch black stage; he cannot find his own mattress. At last he gives up, and hopes to find a trunk to sleep on. But there is someone sleeping on every trunk, and his groping hands wake them, so they curse him. There is nothing for him to do but stop groping. His hands come across the curtain, which trails on the floor, so he lies down on it, but half of his body is on the floor, and he sleeps with his face against the curtain. The curtain has gathered a decade's dust, and his face is now covered in dust, but he feels secure up against it.

They know that it is neither the right time nor the right place, but they cannot control themselves anymore. After such a long rest they are even more robust than before, both mentally and physically. They are experienced and therefore more mature; they know how to reserve their energy for the critical moment. With filthy and sinful yearning gnawing at them, they feel uneasy whatever they do, and have no heart for anything else. But they simply cannot find a quiet place. There are people everywhere, in every hidden corner, and the people are always in groups.

They can only go to the river bank after the show, but even then, they find that it is not so quiet there. People come and go, and there are also tractors, with rude and foul-mouthed country folks sitting on top. A man and a woman walking together is enough to provoke their shameless dirty jokes and sneers. These people, with their particularly good eyesight and keen interest, sweep the willow bushes like search lights; nothing escapes them. Moreover, the nights have never since been as dark as that night; the moon and the stars are always shining brightly now, so that even a small blade of grass is clearly visible. Without the curtain of darkness, even the most secure place has no appeal for them. They have to be on the alert, and they feel ashamed, guilty, and remorseful, so that

they cannot concentrate on enjoying that miraculous moment
of pain and pleasure. In retrospect, that night is as unreal as
a fairy tale. It seems to have been the mysterious working of
fate.

Since someone on a passing tractor roared at them one later
night at the crucial moment, their feelings of despair and
shame have kept them from the river bank. The mere mention of the river bank brings shame and embarrassment, so
they try to hold out in the small, crowded theatre, and only
they themselves know how intense their suffering is. They feel
that there is nothing but pain in the world, nothing but the
hardship of endurance. They feel that if they have to continue
this hopeless endurance, then life itself will become a burden
for them. They are only prolonging a life that has neither value
nor joy; what use is such a life to them? And yet they are
young, and therefore will not give up so easily. They do their
utmost to look for chances to be alone together.

The finale to the show is a dance in which almost all the
girls have to perform. Though she does not have to go on stage,
she has to help the principal dancer change costumes in the
middle of the dance. After this costume change the dance goes
on for another seven minutes before the show is finished. Normally the dancers would take off their make-up and change
before they return to the dormitory, but since it is so cramped
back stage, many of the girls prefer to go back to the dormitory
to change, and it takes them at least three minutes to go from
the stage, bypass the audience, get to the back of the theatre
and go upstairs into the projection room. So altogether the
two of them have ten minutes on their own. To them, the
ten minutes are precious. They know by heart every phrase
of the music coming from the stage through the windows of
the projection room. For them, every phrase is a landmark,
reminding them of what they should do. There is a tight

schedule for everything. When the fervour subsides, they feel completely despondent, so much so that they want to hit their heads against the wall until they bleed. But when the next day comes, their burning desire drives any sense of shame away.

"What are we doing?"

They are still panting, but must get up at once. He rushes downstairs, and she speedily tidies up the battlefield. Puzzled and distraught, she thinks:

"What are we doing?"

She is never much of a thinker, but the sense of shame and desperation has actually driven her to question herself:

"What are we doing?"

But there is no answer to the question. They cannot answer it themselves, and no one can answer it for them, so they continue to blame themselves and suffer.

Because of the lack of time and the tension they cannot attain complete ecstasy, which as a result becomes more alluring than ever. As they are deeply disturbed by the presence of the others, they feel even more lonely, and so they stick together, cosseting each other and looking on the whole world with enmity. He has to give her something every day: cologne, ice-cream, a handkerchief, hair pins, face powder .... Every day she sits at the mirror powdering herself. A thick layer of white powder on her dark complexion makes her look like a dried, powdered persimmon. She thinks she is pretty, but she has no heart to rejoice. She is just too sad to pay attention to anything. Because of this sadness, she has become tender and considerate.

She goes to the market for some eggs and fresh meat, then cooks for him on a borrowed stove. She puts in too little oil, and there's no salt, but he still eats it all up with gratitude. She sits by his side, looking at him eagerly, waiting for a response. He eats in silence, not saying a word. She watches

as he slowly finishes the food, and she relaxes, feeling satisfied.
They cannot find a place where they can talk alone, but their
souls have sworn eternal faithfulness to each other thousands
of times. They are agitated and helpless, suffering both
physically and mentally. Yet far from becoming worn and hag-
gard, they are more robust and more energetic than ever. They
are pushed to the limit of their endurance, but they must hold
on. It is as though a fire is scorching their hearts, and they
have nowhere to hide, so they just hold their heads up and
stand there and let the fire burn them alive. Nothing can be
more painful than this.

In the evenings, the sound of sirens from the ferries comes
to them from the direction of the pier, and they think that
it is a ferry from their small town. They are then seized by
a mad, uncontrollable urge to go back, to leave the hubbub
of this place behind. When they think about it now, their small
town is so quiet and peaceful.

Fortunately, the troupe has finished all its performances at
this venue, and is going to move on to its next stop. They
look forward to the new place eagerly, hoping that there they
will find a quiet corner to indulge their burning desire.

This time the troupe travels by train. Patiently they wait
for everything on stage to be dismantled and put into trunks,
for the scenery, lighting equipment, props and costumes to
be loaded onto an open carriage booked by the troupe, and
then wait for the train on the open platform with the mid-
day sun beating down on them. The train finally arrives, and
they squeeze in. They cannot find a seat, so they have to stand
in the aisle, and even then they are not left to stand in peace.
They must make way for all the trolleys that pass by; if it is
not the trolleys delivering meals then it is the ones carrying
hot water. And if they push against the legs of the seated
passengers they are told off brusquely. But they remain

patient, suppressing their anger because they have such
fervent hopes for the next stop. They have even begun to feel
happy. They stand opposite each other, leaning against the
back of the seats on either side, but they have turned their
faces away from each other. Despite that, they are hoping for
the same thing, and understand each other without resorting
to words. The train rattles on, stopping at every tiny station,
but they are patient enough. They really think that everything
will be fine when they get to their next stop. The river bank
recedes rapidly into the distance; neither of them thinks about
it, yet neither of them can forget it. It will stay with them
forever, always following them, like a threat.

It is an excruciatingly hot summer, and they are pouring
with sweat. At last they have arrived, and get down from the
train thoroughly exhausted. The theatre boasts a thousand seats
but only a tiny courtyard, on three sides of which are single-
storied houses, and in the middle, a pump well. The sound
of running water never stops, as if it is always raining. The
heat of the sun penetrates the thin roof tiles, and the houses
are as hot as ovens. The men, unable to stand the heat, take
their straw mattresses out to sleep in the courtyard, so the courtyard is filled with people.

Only now are they surprised by their former expectations.
What were their expectations founded on? What really had
they been expecting? Did they really think that every one
would have a room of his own? Now that they realize how
absurd and groundless their hope had been, they are even more
depressed. This place is actually worse than the last. Previous-
ly at least people were separated into different sections and
different levels in the theatre, now they are all herded together
in the same place; it is so open, there is nowhere you can hide.
They feel that everything is done in broad daylight and under

the eyes of all the others. Even that river bank, by no means safe, is no longer available to them. They cannot help but remember with regret the city they have just left. All of a sudden it occurs to them that there were so many chances they missed and so many opportunities they wasted. Now that they are here, there is nothing they can do, nothing they can hope for. Disappointed and despondent, they dare not expect anything from the next few stops, and the days seem to drag on endlessly. They are desperate; having lost all hope they become extremely irritable.

On the night they arrived she quarrelled with someone over something really trivial. She was trying to hang up her mosquito net when someone knocked against her, so that the net, just put up, fell down again. In such confusion it is only natural that people would knock against each other unintentionally, and yet she started wailing and howling, her voice so hoarse and choked with tears that she was unable to speak properly. The other girl was not someone to be put upon, and she fought back. Once the girl got worked up she was easily outclassed. The girl used the vilest words and dropped the most obvious hints, so obvious that stupid as she was, she understood them, and yet she had no way of answering back. So she shook and howled like an animal. If people had not held onto her she would probably have thrown herself on the clever girl and torn her to pieces.

From the experience of this first encounter she realizes that she is no match for others. Words do not serve her well; what she says is always weak and stupid. Moreover, since that fight all the girls stay away from her. And yet while they avoid her they deliberately say within her hearing: "If we have no right to provoke her at least we have the right to keep away from her." Anger chokes her, but she has no cause to argue with them. The flame of anger mounts in her heart, merging with her burning desire. She must find an outlet.

She can only lash out at him; it is a call for help. He responds immediately, and the fight starts at once. In his heart a fire has been scorching him, and he would have fought a thousand times with hundreds of people had he not checked himself. After all he is much more rational than her and knows how to control himself. But the scorching fire is burning more fiercely and more cruelly for him than for her; he is at the limit of his endurance. The burning fire has driven him to a dead end. Even if she had not started it all, he would have broken out at that time; it is also a call for help. For him, she provides the only outlet, and for her he is similarly the only outlet. Since there is no other way out they can only fight between themselves.

It is a fight rarely seen in the history of the troupe. He tramples her underfoot so hard that she is almost suffocated. Yet somehow she manages to crawl up from the ground and pounces on him. He falls to the ground, and she picks up a stone and hits him right on the head. There is no sound, and then blood streams down onto the stone slabs. People around them are stunned, and grab her by the waist; she, too, is stunned. They carry him to the hospital but on the way he struggles free and insists on walking back, covering his wound with one hand. Blood trickles down from his hand on to his bare chest. But he feels relaxed and more at peace. On this day they both feel at peace, and the fire in their hearts burns less fiercely.

But from then on they become deadly enemies, bearing each other the deepest malice. It is almost impossible for them to be together on their own. A mere brush will lead to a disastrous fight; the exchange of a few words will see them throwing themselves on one another, and however hard the others try they cannot separate them; they are like two copulating dogs.

It has occurred to a lot of the others that this is an apt analogy, but no one dares say it aloud because it is too crude, and besides, they are really a bit afraid. So they try to separate the two of them in order to avoid conflict. But they just cannot stand being apart. If they do not see each other for a single day they start looking for each other as if they are under a spell. And when they lay eyes on each other they rush forward and start hitting and kicking. And so an unforeseen battle commences.

It is a real battle. Her arms are entwined in his; her legs are entwined in his; her neck is pressed against his. It is a tense and prolonged contest of strength. At first she is on top of him, then he reverses the positions; then she comes on top again, and then again he reverses it. There is no victory, no final result. They try their best to hurt each other; they also wish fervently to be hurt. It is as if they will not be satisfied until they feel the pain, and when they feel it they scream their hearts out. The noise is ear-shattering and it scares the hell out of the others. But the more sensitive ones notice that the horror in their screaming lies precisely in the strange sense of pleasure hidden in it. Having gone through such intensive hardening in combat their bodies have become stronger and less sensitive to pain, and so they have to use more force in order to hurt. They both understand each other's need, and they attack each other's most sensitive and weakest parts. It seems that neither will ever be satisfied until the other dies in their hands, and at the same time they look as if they are ready to die, without regret.

More and more they are losing control. There is no sense left in them, and they try their best to pick a quarrel just as if they were provoking each other's lust. Their entwined bodies rub against each other, as if in a passionate caress. They hate each other. There is no reason for it, but even the thought

of the other makes them explode in anger. Such hate! It goes
to the bone! Their hatred is not rational, and all the stronger
for that reason. When they are rolling on the floor, tearing
at one another, they frequently forget where they are and forget
that they are surrounded by other people watching them. They
are in a feverish hallucination, and if the others try to stop
them they feel that they are interfering with their enjoyment,
and their anger and resentment mount. But they know that
their anger and violence can only be aimed at one person, so
they try even harder to make each other suffer. Of this, they
are clearly aware. How they suffer for it! And yet they cannot
talk to anyone about their suffering. They simply do not
understand the violent force that manipulates them and drives
them on; where does it come from? They do not understand
this fire that is searing them so cruelly; where does it come
from? They do not understand what is happening to them.
What is happening to them? What is happening to them?

In their bodies, a certain consciousness is being stimulated,
being played with; they are spared no pity. They were such
innocent children, what is this that is destined to push them
down into a dark, filthy abyss? It seems that they have fallen
into a trap, a plot, a frame-up. They can't extricate themselves,
and they don't get any assistance. No one will help them. No
one can help them!

They can only use their painful experience to save
themselves; they can only rely on themselves!

The hope of going back seems so remote. There are a dozen
stops waiting for them yet; the contracts were all signed six
months ago. Huge red seals mark the written words, as in-
violable as the law. Of course no one can change this for the
sake of the unknown passions of two unknown children. They
can only wait, and the waiting is endless, with absolutely no
chance for the least pleasure.

There is a difference between every city and every theatre. Some are bigger, some smaller; some better, some worse. But one thing they have in common is the lack of a quiet corner where they can be alone. The river bank with its curtain of willow trees is farther and farther from them. They can no longer see it, but it has left an indelible mark on their memory. So has the siren travelling upstream, bringing them news of the small town they know so well. Unable to put up with their thirst, they can only torture each other in order to give an outlet to their excess physical and sexual energy. Gradually people become used to their fights and no longer try to stop them or pull them apart. Left to fight on their own, without the others pulling and tugging at them, they seem to have lost a certain pleasure. Since they don't have to fight against outside forces, their feverish energy does not have an adequate outlet. Their energy, aimed at each other, is fierce enough to kill. Even they themselves are afraid now, for deep in their hearts they know how much the other means to them. Oh, if they lose each other what are they going to do? So without being aware of it they restrain themselves a little.

The weather is extremely hot, and the heat in the air merges with the heat in their hearts, making them feel as though they would die. Death would actually be a blessing, he thinks. And though she does not have the wisdom to contemplate matters of life and death, she is not afraid of death either. But their youthful life is so robust, so invincible, and so well trained that they are almost immortal. A layer of acne has exploded on his face and body, like ripened fruit, ready to burst any time. As for her, she has not lost weight under such torture; on the contrary she has grown even fatter, and the weight she has put on shows in the most unflattering places. Her figure has changed. In the old days, although she was not well-proportioned, she neverthess looked like a young girl; there was a quiet prettiness about her. Now she looks doltish, like a country woman, her buttocks hanging heavily over her legs as she swaggers along, like a duck. She looks filthier every day, paying no attention to the way she dresses, and yet she still powders herself. She pays no attention to her manners either. Flipping up the rear of her crumpled-up skirt, she sits down, and when she gets up her sweat has left a mark on the chair; it is the shape of her buttocks. A well-meaning girl had a word with her, but she did not pay much attention, and soon forgot all about it.

"She looks like a woman," the girls say behind her back. And then a married woman says decisively:

"She *is* a woman."

This heat is really too much. No one can sleep on the huge beds meant for a dozen people anymore. The men have long decided to sleep in the open, and now the women also move out of the dormitory one by one, and sleep on the flat roof of the theatre. The men and the women each keep to one side of the roof. Though in the second half of the night their bodies are soaked with dew, no one can pluck up the courage to go indoors.

Inside the room it is pitch black. The mosquitoes' earth-shaking humming is like a thousand violins, all played with loosened strings. Deep in the night, without signalling to each other in advance, they come down stealthily from the roof and go into the deserted room. The mosquitoes zoom about blindly, bands of them dashing against their faces, hands and bodies. They stand there quietly; all they can hear is each other's panting. After standing there for a while he grabs her by the shoulders and pushes her inside someone's mosquito net. The mosquitoes follow them in, humming in their ears, bombarding them. They feel the itchy, burning sensation in dozens of spots all over their bodies, but they don't care about that now. They are sweating profusely, rolling and turning in a pool of filthy, stinking sweat. The straw mattress has been removed and the bed planks are rough, crushing against their bones, scratching their skin, thrusting hundreds of splinters into their bodies. But they don't feel anything. All of a sudden the mosquitoes stop their bombardment; the heat recedes and they actually feel fresh and cool. But it lasts only a split second. Then come shame and remorse. She starts sobbing, tears streaming down her face. Though he does not cry, he is thoroughly dejected and is crying in his heart.

God! Are they going to die of this? Is this an incurable disease? Should they go to a doctor or ask the opinion of others? But it is so shameful! This is a secret they must keep from everyone! Because the secret must be guarded, they will never come out of their loneliness and isolation. They will always have this vile secret; they will never be able to get on naturally with others; they will always be isolated! He punches the edge of the bed with his fist, not daring to make any noise. Thousands of mosquitoes surround them inside the net, making a feast of their blood. They are completely numb, no longer aware of any pain or itching. The world is drowned in a thunderous moaning and they have completely lost their bearings.

In the cool autumn they return to the small town. Towards evening the luxuriant green trees come into view, with the sun sinking gradually behind them, casting a golden glow around them. The colour of the trees gradually darkens, finally turning into a black mass concealed in the darkening twilight. The ferry finally docks when the sky is completely dark. The troupe disembarks; all its members exhausted, carrying their luggage on their shoulders and crossing the narrow gangway to shore. The water-men are still singing. Their winding, drawn-out tunes float in the darkness between water and sky, travelling a long way.

The two of them cross the quivering gangway in the midst of the crowd. The gangway shifts underneath their feet, but it will never throw them into the water. They know this quivering sensation very well, and yet all of a sudden it has become unfamiliar to them. They lift their chins slightly; their faces are worn-out and not even the darkness of the night can conceal that. They look coldly at this small town which they have not seen for three months, and cannot but feel a little sad. Everything looks so familiar, and yet everything seems to be estranged from them. They reach the bank and stop for a minute. Not far from them there is a water-cart trying to climb the steep river bank. The water-man ducks his head and his deep voice lingers powerfully on the lower notes of his song. The cart rocks, and water is spilled from the tanks. The road leading to the main street lies ahead, illuminated by moonlight. There are a few pedestrians and a cart drawn by a donkey whose shoes strike the earthen road with a sharp, drumming sound. The two of them walk onto the road. Though it leads to the main street there are also several paths branching out, leading to far off places beyond where the eye can see. The donkey cart goes on one such path and disappears, but the sharp drumming sound can still be heard for a long time.

The road leads to the main street. The doors of the shops and houses on the street are all closed; all is quiet. The footsteps of the group disturb the silence. Someone opens a door slightly to take a look; they can make out that this person, half hidden behind the door, wears nothing but a garment of some kind draped around the shoulders. The lights in the display window of the photographer's have been put out, but the same coloured pictures are still on display. Most are of the girls in the troupe, with dewy red lips and thick, black rims painted around their eyes. There is also a picture of her, not coloured, left in a corner. It is a picture of her in the role of "Xier"[2] and her head is turned in an innocent yet affected manner. When the two of them walk past the window they can't help looking in. These things seem to belong to a distant past; it even seems that the person in the photograph is someone they do not know very well. They glance at it coldly, and walk on.

The paving stones they walk on are bathed in moonlight. The smooth stones reflect the light and it seems that the outline of every stone has been traced out in ink. If you keep your eyes on the road for a long time, it doesn't look like a road paved with stones, but a net of criss-crossing lines. They walk on this net, as if walking in a dream, a very peaceful dream. They walk in a trance. Yet everything around them seems so real; the road is so hard that you can hear every footfall. The moonlight streams down their bodies, cool and yet warm. By the roadside there are slippery pieces of persimmon peel; if you step on them, you will slip. The stove outside the front door of the small restaurant is still hot, and there are still sparks of fire. The toilet by the roadside stinks, but the smell has spread such a long way that no one is bothered by it anymore.

"We're back at last," they think.

"We're finally back," they think.

But deep at heart they feel strangely quiet, and a little disappointed. They seem to have lost something, left something behind. They are like two strangers walking into this small town they know. The last three months have been as long as thirty, no, three hundred years. And yet the town remains unchanged. At most there are a few more wild cats, but they are quiet, scurrying about noiselessly, or perching on top of

---

[2] A character in the dance *The White-haired Woman*.

walls watching the humans. A low wall has just been pulled down and the new house is not yet finished. So half a new house sits quietly in the midst of tiles and rubble.

At last they come to the theatre. The front door is wide open and the lights are shining brilliantly: lights in the gate house, lights in the pantry, lights in the kitchen, and lights in the rooms of married members of the troupe. The gate keeper stands waiting by the door. They walk into the courtyard amidst this warm welcome and return to their dormitories. Doors are opened, then windows, and then the lights are turned on one after another. Even the lights in the studio are all turned on.

They go through the studio to the kitchen for a snack, and as they walk on the faded red floor, the floor boards move slightly and creak. They cannot help standing in front of the mirror for a while, and what they see in the mirrors seems unfamiliar. She is still so young, and yet the skin under her eyes is puffy, her complexion extremely coarse and the pores above her lips much larger than before. The way she walks is awkward, like an old goose. He is so thin that his face is all wrinkled up. The scars left by acne cover his whole body. He is dying for a good wash. There is a long queue in front of the wash room, and those who do not want to wait take some water back to their dormitories to wash, splashing water all over the floor. From the first floor the water seeps through the rotted floor boards and drips down to the ground floor. People on the ground floor shout and scream as the water showers on them, but no quarrel ensues. Everyone is happy to be back at last! For a hundred days they have wandered about like homeless people, and now they are finally back in this peaceful nest. They are happy.

The two of them are happy too, but they are much quieter. In the three months they have been away they kept wanting

to come back, as if back here there were another world, another
kind of life. But now that they are back, they do not see what
is new in the life that awaits them. Of course now it is much
easier for them to be together. They know every corner of this
place and they know where to find a quiet spot; they can name
ten such quiet spots offhand. Isn't it true that when they were
away, all they had longed for was somewhere where they could
be alone and put all inhibitions aside and do those most
shameless things they revel in? Now they can find such a place,
but how they have suffered! Their suffering has turned this
long dreamt-of day into something banal.

Yet on the second evening after their return, they slip out.
There is no need to talk about it; over this they have a firm
implicit understanding. From then on they go out almost every
night, and do not return until midnight. Sometimes they do
not even wait till midnight, but just return after they have
finished. To them it is as commonplace as eating, drinking
and sleeping; there is no special meaning to it, and yet it is
indispensable. They can only live like this; it seems that there
is no other way. They seem to be driven by an overwhelming
force, and once the routine is established they are powerless
to break it.

But their joy has dwindled; it lasts only for a split second,
sometimes not even that. Now they are agitated, because they
seem to have lost something which is of vital importance to
them, and they must have it back. They try repeatedly and
desperately, not giving up until they have thoroughly exhausted themselves. They just do not understand what human
beings are supposed to live for. Is it only for something so base,
something for which the punishment is pain and remorse?
They seem to have fallen into a trap camouflaged as a green
lawn with pretty flowers, and now they cannot stop their fall
into the abyss. They seem to have slipped into seething cur-

rents and are caught in a whirlpool; they are no longer in control. They feel that they are the most unfortunate people in the world and wish that with death, they could put an end to it all. Yet they cannot make up their minds, for there is actually something they still cherish, and what they cherish is also what brings them pain — that vile pleasure. It seems that they have not yet lived through all their predestined sufferings, and for them there is no escape.

Winter follows in the wake of autumn, and it is an exceptionally mild winter. It has not snowed much, just a thin layer which melts as soon as it touches the ground. Crystal snowflakes turn immediately to pitch black mire. And then spring follows, a spring of diseases. Almost everyone is ill — flu, stomach aches, coughs, asthma, and hepatitis B, which has spread all of a sudden. Moreover there is a strange illness from which no one is exempted — diarrhoea. At first it is just a watery emission, then slight diarrhoea, and then towards the end the patient will have a slight fever, after which the disease completes its course. There is no major consequence, but for a fortnight you feel weak and lose your appetite. The doctors at the local hospital rack their brains; after consulting all the medical books they are still unable to find the answer. Finally they discover that it is the drinking water.

There is no tap water in town, and the water pumped from the wells is bitter, so everyone drinks water from the river. All the year round boats and ferries run on the river, and the ferries are fuelled by diesel oil which leaks into the river. If you look dispassionately at the river you can see shiny patches of oil, as if a layer of skin has grown on the water. Since the winter was mild, many of the bacteria were not killed by the cold, and there are even some new and active varieties. So the water is exceptionally dirty. Everyone drinks that water, so everyone has diarrhoea; it would be a wonder if this were not the case.

The hospital makes up a special herbal prescription. A table is placed outside the hospital entrance, and anyone with diarrhoea will get a packet of herbs; there is no need for registration. Anyone who works in town needs only submit a claim form; for those who don't, and for the villagers, the fee is only five cents.

Few villagers suffer from the disease. "Not fortunate enough to drink the water of the main street," they say gaily, seemingly rejoicing in others' misfortune. But the villagers are kind at heart and really pity the people in town. These days the villagers come into town with much greater frequency, riding in their wagons on which are placed black synthetic leather sacks for collecting night soil. The toilets in town are rapidly filled, and within hours after they have been emptied, yellowish liquid overflows again from the toilet into the street. Even the cats and dogs have caught the disease, but no one gives them medicine, and they have dirtied the whole street. You can see sick-looking cats and dogs all over the place, dragging their feet, walking with their tails between their legs. A nice, quiet town is turned overnight into a stinking, filthy place. It is as if a crime against heaven has been committed and this is the retribution allotted to it.

Even at times like this they are still unable to put a stop to it. They have to walk a long way in search of a spot unsullied by excrement. They walk all the way to the fields some ten miles from town and hide themselves amongst the bundles of straw, which are treasures in the eyes of the villagers who use it as cow-feed. They crush the straw to bits.

This night, weak from diarrhoea, they have actually fallen asleep amidst the straw bundles. It is a disturbed night for them. Both have nightmares which seem so real that they break out in cold sweat. The straw which they use as a cover is soaked through with dew, the wetness penetrating to their clothes and bodies so that they shiver from the cold. But they are not awoken. They just curl up tightly, sometimes sleeping close together, sometimes rolling apart. After a very long time they open their eyes almost simultaneously, and see that it is nearly dawn. They look at the pale white sky with incomprehension, dazed. And then they suddenly realize that they have spent the whole night here. They exclaim in horror, and then rush back into town. Farmers who get up early catch sight of this young man and young woman with bits of broken straw hanging on their heads and clothes, and stare at them in surprise as they run past. From afar the bell of a production team strikes a morning call for the workers — dong, dong, dong; the sound reverberates in the air. To them it is a sound of misfortune, but they do not have time to think about that now.

By the time they get back to the theatre, panting, everyone is up. Some are washing and brushing their teeth by the water basin, some are squatting against the wall having breakfast, and others are already practising in the studio. Those eating and washing chat and share jokes, and from the studio comes the sound of recordings of piano music used for practice. It is a fresh and beautiful melody in 2/2. It seems that this scene has been carefully arranged and people are making a display of their happiness. In face of such bliss, pure and peaceful, the two of them are shocked and ashamed. They feel that they are the most unfortunate people in the world. In the evening, she comes to the decision that it is better to die.

She is a simple-minded child. When she came as a young student to the ballet troupe she only had three years of schooling behind her, and couldn't even write a proper letter to her parents in a neighbouring province. But she was a happy child who knew no problems or worries, and was concerned with nothing but eating and sleeping. That was why although she was many times more diligent than the others in her practice, she never made much progress. Just as life seemed to her a simple matter, so now she thinks death, too, is simple. For her, there is no difficulty in making the decision to die. She vaguely feels that death is just like sleep, like setting off on a long journey to a far away place. Of course setting off to die is different from the other kind of setting off, in that she will not be able to bring anything along, no matter how fond she is of it. She must leave everything behind. Well, she will leave everything if it must be so, it doesn't really matter, she thinks in her simple-mindedness.

But when she really begins to plan for her death, she realizes that to leave her things in order is not easily done. As is her habit before she sets off on a journey, she packs her clothes first. She gets out her big rattan hamper and throws everything inside on the bed; then she shakes the clothes out one by one, smoothes them and then folds them up tidily, thinking all the while to whom she should give these clothes. She finds some old clothes which she wore when she first joined the troupe; they are very small and old-fashioned. She measures these against herself, and just cannot believe that she once wore them. Seen against her body these just look like baby clothes. She remembers she was only twelve then. Thinking of herself at twelve, she feels that was a very long time ago, but in fact only nine years have passed. While handling these clothes she notices the hemlines, sewn by her mother on a Butterfly sewing machine. She seems to hear the light-hearted rattle of the sewing machine, like a song. A pity that these clothes are too old and look too awful; who'd want them now? No one. Just one look at the bright red and green patterns is enough to turn anyone away. Of course the villagers are the exception; they'd want anything. She recalls the time when the troupe went to perform at a waterworks construction site.

In the house where they stayed, the daughter of the family did not even have a pair of pants and had to sit in bed all day, covering herself with a quilt just like a fish net woven of cotton thread. So she gets hold of a piece of paper and wraps the clothes up. On it she writes: I hope the leader will give this to the children of poor peasants.

She places the packet in a corner of the hamper and continues packing. She has kept the military-style clothes with bell-bottom pants that were in fashion some time ago, and though they are old, they are still quite presentable. They are now too narrow around the waist so she can no longer wear them. She can give them to her sister, who is two years younger and has started working as a shopkeeper in a butcher's after graduating from middle school. Though these clothes are no longer in fashion, most folks consider theatre people trend setters in fashion, and she remembers how envious her sister was when she saw these clothes. So she wraps them up and writes on the packet: To my dear sister. She does not know why she has put the word "dear" in front of "sister", and suddenly she wants to cry. Her sister was never "dear" to her. There was one time when her sister came to see her, but she had asked for home leave, and they missed each other on the way. Her room-mate took over the responsibility of taking care of her sister, and took her meal coupons, which she put in a box on the window ledge, to buy the best dishes for her sister. She came back after five days and found the box containing her meal coupons empty. She berated her sister, who left the same night. She had started working early and therefore had a special status at home; she had never thought much of her sister.

She places the packet in the hamper and continues packing. She sees her favourite overcoat, rust coloured, which she had asked someone to bring to her from the provincial capital.

It fits her perfectly. It has a low-cut Western-style collar, and though this is commonly seen in the cities, it is considered extremely fashionable in the small town. The girls had been full of admiration and had tried their best to talk her into selling it. Of course she hadn't; she likes it too much.

She likes it too much to give it away, so she decides to keep it for herself, and with it she'll wear her black pant-suit and the leather shoes with T-straps. This is her best and favourite suit. In it, she looks a different person.

She packs her things one by one, and strangely every item triggers her memory. She had not realized that she has so much to remember; it makes her sad. Suddenly she does not want to die, well, she has not stopped wanting to die altogether, just today, she does not feel like dying today. Tomorrow! While she locks the hamper she thinks of her meal coupons and money, which she decides to send home. Her meal coupons amount to over a hundred catties. She had not collected them for three months and when she finally went for them the accountant said, ''I'll give you the kind you can use nation-wide.'' So now she has over a hundred catties' worth of nation-wide coupons. She did not know that she could use special registered mail to send meal coupons home, and she was afraid that they would get lost in the post, so she has kept them with her to take home next time. But now she can no longer wait.

She heaves a sigh and pushes the hamper under the bed. She then smoothes the bedsheet. She feels that she should also do something about the sheet, the mattress and the quilt. She must wash them; she has not done that for a few months, and now she finally notices the smell. She finds that there is still a lot to be done, so her heart is at ease; she simply cannot die today. After dinner, she thinks that she should take a look at the surroundings of the place where she is going to die,

so after washing her own bowl and chopsticks she asks her
room-mate to take them back to the dormitory and goes out
alone.

She has chosen a spot by the river. She follows the slightly
sloping main road until she sees the ferry pier and the ticket
office with a tiled roof. As the road leads down to the river
bank it becomes steep. She cannot control her steps, which
leads her to run, and the momentum is so great that she almost
runs into the river. She stops herself at once, and at that moment a water-man's song suddenly rises in the air. For some
reason the water-man is singing very resoundingly, a sound
which would make anyone's soul tremble. She just stands there
while the water-man sings louder and louder, as if he is trying with all his might to shout himself hoarse. All of a sudden it occurs to her that if by tomorrow, when she is really
going to die, the water-man still howls like that, how can she
go in peace? So she walks along the bank in search of a spot
where she would not hear the water-man's song.

As the troupe takes dinner early, the sun has just set and
the river is a palette of brilliant colours. She walks along this
brilliant and colourful river as dusk deepens, enshrouding the
rapid currents and her silhouette, but the water-man's song
is still reverberating in the sorrowful evening. She cannot get
away; the water-man's song follows her, but stubbornly she
walks on.

Meanwhile, he is anxiously waiting in their old meeting
place. She's never missed a date before. Besides, it is not really a "date"; they both come by instinct. He does not know
what has happened to her, and as the moon rises he starts to
look for her in another of their old haunts. Maybe she has gone
there. But there is no one there either, only the wind whistling as it blows desolately over the grass. He hurries on to a
third place .... He will not want to die because he is a much

more complicated person, more intelligent and rational than her. He knows what a terrible thing death is. He would much rather drag out this life than put a clean end to it. He runs alone in the whistling wind from one spot to another. Finally he thinks of the river bank. Though he thinks of the river bank in this town, in his mind's eye he sees the river bank upstream lined by curtains of willow trees. He is not particularly hopeful as he runs towards the river bank, and when he gets there, she is gone.

No matter how far she walks she cannot get away from the water-man's song, alternatingly high-spirited and tender. She turns back in a temper and they just miss each other. It is the first time they have missed each other, and he does not know that he has just missed her by chance; he thinks that he will never find her again. She has always been waiting as he expected and moving in his direction; and he has always been waiting as she expected and moving in her direction. But this time it is different, and he knows that there must be an important reason for this, but he does not know what it is. He is enveloped in a sense of foreboding, not knowing whether fortune or misfortune lies ahead. He just feels a little afraid, a little hollow and a little dejected. The water-man's song has died away now, and the only sound is that of the water lapping against the bank.

By now she is already fast asleep. For a very long time she has not had such pure and peaceful sleep, undisturbed by dreams. When she opens her eyes it is still early and the light in the sky is hazy, but she feels refreshed and in good spirits. Her body is warm, dry and smooth, so she notices the greasiness of the sheet and the quilt cover. She thinks of all the things she has to do on this day, and decides that she cannot just lie there, so she gets up and takes the sheet and quilt cover off to wash. Both are completely black, and feel thick and soft to the touch, as if they are covered with oil. The clear water pumped up from the well splashes on the bed sheet and quilt cover; she rubs them with her hands and submerges them totally in the water. Then she starts to soap them, using up half a bar of soap. When she pours some hot water on the washing and rubs it over the scrubbing board, it becomes foamy immediately. The foam warms her hands, and light-heartedly she rubs the washing against the scrubbing board, making a slopping sound with every push. This is nice! she suddenly thinks, and feels quite happy.

While she is washing the sheets he comes by, carrying a basin, his face all gloomy, and asks her in a low voice why she did not turn up the night before. She replies: Terrible stomach ache. He believes her, and yet he does not believe. He asks whether she will be there tonight. Yes, she says. She is going to die today anyway, she thinks, so she can be irresponsible and tell any lie she likes. He does not really believe her, and stealing a glance at her he finds that she looks very peaceful. This look disturbs him, but he cannot go on questioning her because the old man has come to clean the kettles.

She goes on rubbing the quilt cover happily, and the snowy foam is splashed all over the place. There are also tiny bubbles which reflect the light of the rising sun, turning themselves into the colour of rainbows and floating gracefully away in the air. She actually starts to sing. Her voice is low, but not coarse, and after listening for some time you may even find it quite tuneful. She is humming as she washes the quilt cover buried in a basin of snowy foam. Her sleeves are pulled up, and her dark strong arms are pushed into the foam. She feels incredibly clean and warm. She can feel the strength of her own arms; she scrubs and washes a whole basin of sheets as though they are handkerchiefs, not feeling at all tired. When she has finished scrubbing, she rinses the sheet and the quilt cover, and they look unexpectedly clean and white. After rinsing, she hangs them up to dry. The sun is already high in the sky, and sunlight throws her shadow onto the clean white bed sheet. She sees her own shadow, with arms out-stretched, trying to smooth the sheet, and thinks to herself: "Is this me?" She looks at her shadow; it seems unfamiliar. Then she picks up the basin and runs away. All of a sudden she wants to have a good wash.

She gets herself a lot of water: she fills two basins, one normally used for washing the face and the other for washing the feet, as well as a plastic bucket. She carries these one after another into the wash-room and then shuts the door. In the room it is pitch black but the water is shining. The three rings, which look like three deep wells, surround her. She puts her hands into a basin, and then wets her hair with the hot water. Her greasy scalp is soaked through, and she feels a prickly sensation, a little painful and itchy, but very comfortable too, and she cannot help but shiver. She splashes water on herself with a towel, and the parts of her body which come into contact with the water feel as if they are being pricked by needles, being awakened from prolonged numbness. The skin all over her body has awakened, and all the pores are open, swallowing the scalding water. All the dirt inside her body has flowed out, and she feels completely relaxed. She soaps herself time and again, each time making a richer and cleaner lather. After repeated rubbing, her skin becomes thin, soft and smooth. She dries herself, puts on her clothes, and opens the door. It is almost noon, and the sunlight is piercing, so she narrows her eyes. At this moment she does not want to die. She feels comfortable, and she has never felt this way before, so she decides to wait till the next day.

Dried in the sun, the bed sheet and quilt cover have become soft and smooth, with a fragrant smell of sunlight. Freshly washed, she lies in a clean bed and thinks to herself that she has done the right thing giving herself an extra day. And then she falls asleep in peace. While she is sleeping soundly he is running wildly between their old haunts looking for her, his heart filled with a sense of premonition, not knowing whether fortune or misfortune lies before him. He is fearful and confused, and at the same time tortured by his lust. He grinds his teeth and says to himself: if he ever finds her he will tear her to pieces, grind her to powder. Vaguely he senses that she has betrayed him, that she has betrayed the unspoken trust between them. He feels even angrier. This betrayal is in a sense an escape: it is as if she has abandoned him in this bottomless pit of suffering and escaped herself. How can she be so cruel? How can she leave him to struggle hopelessly alone in the abyss with nothing to hang on to? He runs about in agitation amid the wild grass that comes up to his knees, stepping on dry branches which cut his ankles, and he begins to bleed. This restores a little peace of mind to him, and he sits down dejectedly on the ground, holding his head in both hands. An insect climbs from his foot on to his leg, and he does not even notice. It rests on his leg and starts singing.

She is definitely going to die today, she thinks. She cannot bear it any longer, and there is no reason why she should go on doing so. It is only because she is going to die that she can behave so naturally as she repeatedly lies to him in face of his anger; that she can eat and chat with the others in such perfect bliss; that she even feels equal with the others. She has been relieved of all her mental burdens simply because she is going to die. She had never thought that the decision to die would make her so happy, and she comforts herself with the thought that she has made the right decision. But since she is so relaxed and happy she feels that it is a pity to die

now, and keeps on procrastinating, thus extending her enjoyment of this happiness. She washes herself every day, and
makes herself neat and tidy. Since she does not want to dirty
herself she instinctively suppresses her desire. Yet she still feels
ashamed, as if she has cheated someone.

On this day, she finally decides to die. In the evening she
walks alone to the river bank. It is all quiet. The ferry has come
and gone, the ticket office with a red-tiled roof has closed,
and everyone has left. The water-men are taking a rest and
have stopped singing. She walks along the bank for a while,
and then stands still. There is no moon, nor stars, and the
pitch black river is rolling by, like a huge animal breathing
slowly and heavily. She is suddenly afraid, and shivers. Then
the moon jumps out from behind the clouds, and a water-
man's song, loud and clear, rises into the air. She shakes un-
controllably and feels extremely frightened. Only now does
she understand that death is no simple matter; it is not a simple matter at all. If she dies she will never live again; if she
leaves she will never be able to come back. And she cries. Tears
roll down her cheeks and the water-man's song has become
gentle and tender, its echoes lingering on the pitch black river.
Moonlight illuminates everything, and the shadows of the
willow trees along the banks are dancing gracefully. Must she
die?

She asks herself, must she die?

She asks herself in tears, can she not go on living? It is nice
like this! She is in total despair, and so she cries in despair.

Can she not die? She begs of herself. She will be good; she
will behave herself. When there is no answer she can only cry
pitifully.

At the same time but in a different place — the patch of
wild grass where they frequently met — he too is crying pitifully on his own. Now he finally understands that she has cheated

him, that she has abandoned him. How can she do that? He is so weak, so pitiful. He cries so hard that he rolls about on the ground, and the stones and withered branches cut into him, but he does not even feel them, and remains sad and tearful. He does not know how he is going to bear the days to come; life is like an endless dark night, and he cannot see the light of dawn. How can she be so heartless! They should suffer together; they must suffer together; what else can they do?

She is crying on the bank, sitting close to the water's edge, holding her legs, with her head buried between her knees. The water-man's song rises and falls, as if it is calling for a lost child; the moon hides behind the clouds, then comes out again, as if it is showing her the way home.

He buries his head in the thick wild grass, covering himself with the dark grass. He wails in the pitch black darkness, over the lonely days ahead when he will have to suffer on his own.

Like a thief she steals back into the courtyard and then into her own room, feeling all the while that she has no right to be back here again and is therefore very much ashamed of herself. And yet her disgraceful stomach complains of hunger and actually starts rumbling. There is nothing for it but to take out half a piece of steamed bread left over from dinner, and chew on it in embarrassment. She is embarrassed to be still alive; it is as if she has stolen this life of hers. After chewing at the bread for some time, she can taste its sweetness, and her stomach settles down, so she gets into bed quietly, thinking all the while how she is to face the others when the new day dawns.

Yet when the next day comes, everyone treats her the same as before; she cannot detect the slightest difference in their behaviour towards her. She is both surprised and grateful and becomes particularly diligent, fetching hot water for her

room-mate and helping the gate-keeper to sweep the
courtyard. When water in the tea kettle boils, it is she who
runs to fetch the "boiled water" plaque and place it on the
kettle. The day passes uneventfully. And just as she starts to
feel secure, she comes across him outside the kitchen.

She is so scared that she spills the bowl of congee in her
hands. As he has lain in bed in the dormitory the whole day,
she has not seen him nor thought about him throughout the
day. And now it suddenly dawns on her that he is the most
difficult problem. He stares at her balefully and asks what was
the matter with her. She stammmers that it was her stomach
ache again. At that he says, "I'll give you something to ache
about!" and kicks her in the belly. She doubles up; the bowl
in her hands falls to the ground. But she keeps quiet, thinking that she deserves this because she has gone back on her
own decision to die. The others rush forward to hold him
down, and to hold her down, but she does not intend to fight
back at all. She does not even answer back, but just picks up
the pieces of her bowl and runs away.

He struggles aimlessly as the others pull him back, uttering
vile oaths which no one understands. She runs upstairs, into
her own room, and throws herself on her bed. In her heart
she is exclaiming: I won't do it; I won't do it no matter what!
I'll never do that again. I'll do anything to put an end to that!
Her belly hurts a little, for he really kicked hard at her. There
is a slight pain around her belly, and the pain is crawling like
a living thing, teasing her. All of a sudden she is terrified,
for the desire in her body is again on the rise, resurrected by
her decision not to die. As evening comes, she becomes extremely unsettled, knowing that he is waiting for her in the
same old place. She is so agitated that she almost runs there.
She feels like someone with malaria, hot one minute, cold the
next. It is hopeless; she will die of this illness. You mustn't

go, you mustn't! In her heart she thunders this warning at
herself. "Just for the last time, out of pity for him!" a different will in her says. She knows that pitying him is a lie;
she actually pities herself, and she realizes it, but this does
not destroy the will to go, at once weak and strong. Yet she
knows that if she goes there will be no end to it; she will not
be able to put an end to it. Now she suddenly becomes very
rational, as if she understands all the good and evil in the
world. She has grown up in this war of wills. She has not gone
there this night, but she has been extremely disturbed. She
has not gone because she has consoled herself: I'll go tomorrow night.

She is frightened and disturbed the whole of the next day,
but her desire has grown stronger and more active from having been starved in the past few days. When night falls, she
can hold out no longer, and runs there. But there is no trace
of him. She runs to the second place, but he isn't there either.
Then the third place, the fourth, and he is nowhere to be
found. She stamps her feet in frustration and looks all around
her.

He had given up on her the night before and decided not
to come here and wait. Again they have missed each other.
This is the second time they have missed each other and it
seems to confirm that they are destined to part. Sad and at
a loss she walks back to the theatre. The studio is brightly lit,
the piano playing loudly, and there are laughter and songs.
Suddenly she shivers: she was lucky that he wasn't there, really
lucky! She is frightened by what she has done; her heart is
filled with fear, and yet it is also filled with joy. He wasn't
there; it was as though the gods were protecting her.

The water in the river has suddenly become pure, and the
diarrhoea subsides. The obnoxious smell on the street gradually

disperses, and one notices the sweet fragrance of the scholartree blossoms. It is summer now, and this summer the
temperature is just right. Pure sunlight streams down, and the
trees and grass are luxuriantly green. In the countryside, the
vegetables in the fields are big and juicy. In town there are
now a hundred newly arrived cassette-recorders, blaring out
the songs of Hong Kong, Taiwan and mainland singers every
day. One cannot say for sure whether it is the pop songs which
have made cassette-recorders popular, or whether it is the other
way round. When a new shop opens for business, a cassette-
recorder placed at the door sighs about the completely
unrelated subject of the changeable nature of love. Similarly,
a funeral procession walks along to songs broadcast from a
cassette-recorder, also about love. Pop songs always deal with
love, just as popular views of life always deal with love. With
all these love songs the small town is no longer quiet; it has
become noisy. The ferry still calls at the pier twice a day, bringing strange things such as cassette-recorders and Deng Lijun,[3]
and also the gambling tiles, black on one side and white on
the other, which had long disappeared. It also brings other
strange things, such as basketfuls of huge crabs with four
pincers and eight legs. Moreover, it is said that the quiet couple at the secondary school have gone to the other side of the
world, where it is day when it is night here, and night when
it is day here, to live with people with blond hair and blue
eyes. Even the ''wild cats'' who pass through town leave
something behind, such as little bags women put on their
breasts and underpants the size of fists, as well as foreign um-
brellas which can be folded up in three sections. The ''wild
cats'' are doing well now, and all wear glittering watches.

---

[3]A Taiwan singer whose songs were extremely popular in mainland China in
the early and mid-1980s.

Their affair is far from over; he swears he will not let her go so easily. She also feels that being let go by him this way is unreal, and is therefore always a little fearful. What betrays her is her body, which has parted company with her soul and longs fervently to touch his body, to rub against it, even if it means being tortured by him. She would have compromised with the demands of her body had it not been for his gloomy, vicious stare. She knows that he is not going to satisfy her; that he seems to know she is suffering and that she is going to beg his favour, so he becomes extremely proud. Although he is suffering as much as she is, dreaming night after night of amorous acts with this woman, he has decided to take revenge on her and not give her any satisfaction. Their souls are now standing apart from their bodies and engaged in fierce battle.

She has brought all this about, and she almost regrets it; she too dreams frequently of amorous acts with this man. She does not know what is best for her. The hunger of the body is difficult to endure, and there is a regular pattern to it. Every time the crisis comes it is as damaging as a serious illness. Every time it passes she experiences a tremendous sense of relief, and begins to conserve her energy for the next crisis. She actually becomes thinner. But by this time she is no longer interested in the advantages of a slimmer figure — she looks more girlish now — her mind is concentrated on how to repress her physical desire. At times like this she longs to see him; if he were to so much as give her a hint, she would leave all her worries behind and run to him. But he doesn't even look at her. Knowing now that her desire is as strong as his, he makes an effort to suppress himself in order to have her back, all of her. He does not want her to even think of leaving him again. He understands this woman too well; he knows that her robust body needs strong caresses. Since he is predicting that she will soon come crawling to his feet, the sight of her, thin and wan, gives him secret pleasure. Because he is so determined to punish her, he has actually succeeded in suppressing his own physical desire.

Now her resistance is completely dependent on his revenge. If it were not for his desire to punish her she would have totally collapsed and lost her chance to lead a new life. But such resistance is too hard, and too dangerous. She is always afraid that she will find it impossible to endure any longer, and will run to him and grab his legs, and not let go no matter how hard he kicks at her. She has been to the river bank again twice, but death terrified her; her will to live was too strong, and she kept hearing the water-man's song, so she walked back again.

They are at a stalemate. She realizes that he is really angry with her, but he does not understand why she is so stubborn. His will power weakens, and with this weakness the flames of his desire leap and scorch him; it can no longer be suppressed. He begins to watch her movements closely, looking for a chance, and swears to himself that he will get hold of her anyhow. This night, when he catches sight of her going out of the courtyard alone, he follows at a distance.

She crosses the paved main street and walks on to the road which leads to the river bank. In the moonlight the road looks luminously white, sloping gradually down to the river. She walks down the embankment and reaches the river bank, then she walks on along the river. At this moment he quickens his pace and closes on her, but she does not realize that he is there and actually slows down, until she finally comes to a stop. He pounces on her. She is startled, and begins to struggle with all her might. Though she has been longing for this; though she has come to the river bank because she had been tortured by such longing; though her will power is now at its weakest, at the mere touch of his body she is truly terrified, for she realizes that all her past efforts will be proved vain.

She is like someone standing at the edge of a cliff. She can see the clouds floating under her feet, and she knows that beneath the clouds lies an unfathomably deep valley. She is struggling in earnest. But he has completely taken leave of his senses. Like an animal, he is determined to fight to his death. Gradually she weakens, and her struggle becomes ineffective. Because her body has been alone for such a long time; because her desire has been destroyed by hopelessness; because she is really and truly struggling against him; because she is mentally and physically unprepared for this moment, an unexpected, overpowering pleasure sweeps over her. She has never experienced such joy before. She feels that nothing in the past can compare with this, that if she dies now she will have no regrets. The joy fills every cranny of her body; she has never felt so satisfied before, and this satisfaction carries with it a sense of eternity, like a triumphant farewell ceremony. Even he is surprised. Turning over, he lies on the ground by her side, looking at the myriad stars. At this moment, the waterman's song rises from the misty water. It sounds like a hundred men singing in unison, powerful and yet uniform. They lie there side by side, pinned down by a sensation they have never experienced before. They both feel that things have gone awry; it has never been like this before, and they are filled with a sense of premonition.

In the days that follow she feels strange. She begins to crave pickles while getting sick over the meat and fish dishes she normally likes. Sha has been sick several times, and has felt giddy several times, and then she becomes fine again. Even in her worst days her periods had been regular, but now they have stopped, and with this her restless desire has also subsided. She feels that one part of her body is growing heavier by the day, and yet at the same time she feels light-hearted, as though a heavy burden has finally been laid down. At last she understands that she is going to be a mother.

She ties pieces of cloth around her belly so that the others will not detect anything wrong. She has absolutely no common sense and thinks that if she does so the thing will disappear of its own accord. And yet she really loves the life inside her, and is extremely curious about it. At night, she unties the bandages and touches her belly, and she can almost feel the tender body inside. She is calm now, like a smooth lake. It seems that the young life has swallowed or extinguished those flames. Now she is even more afraid of him, afraid that his rough use of her will destroy this life. So she dares not walk on her own, and dares not go anywhere, but stays in the dormitory all the time. She has no thought of what is going to happen; she has not even thought of the fact that this young life will someday come into its own out of the blue. What will people think then? She only keeps close watch as it lies in her belly, and in her undisturbed heart.

As time passes her belly grows bigger and bigger. He is the first to notice it, and he watches her closely, hoping to get a chance to question her about it. This day, she comes downstairs to go to the toilet during the afternoon break, and comes across him in the courtyard. He is squatting outside the studio waiting for her. He asks: "Your belly ..." Before he can finish she says quickly: "It's none of your business," and hurries back into her room. She is afraid that he will hurt it; she will never allow anyone to hurt it. And then the rumours begin to spread, and the leader of the troupe summons her. At first she denies it, and when she realizes that her denials are in vain she admits it. But she refuses to reveal who the

man is and keeps repeating that it is hers alone. This
absurd. The troupe leader mentions his name sinc
has seen what has been going on, but she shakes h
fear: "No, no, no, it's mine, mine alone." And as she says
so she starts crying bitterly. The troupe leader wants her to
have an abortion, but rather than do that she would kill herself
first, and kneels down on the floor begging for mercy. The
troupe leader threatens to dismiss her; she replies that it is
up to him, and actually stops crying.

At this time he is hiding in the dusty props room next to
the office, his face pressed against the wall, stopping his ears
with his hands. On his head hangs a broken spider web. The
walls are peeling, and through the cracks between the bricks
he can hear the conversation next door. He knows that he's
done for, that they are done for! What have they done! He
slides downwards until he sits on the ground all coiled up.
He never doubted that they would be punished for their sin,
but the fact remains that he was thoroughly unprepared for
the day when the punishment came, and had no idea when
it would come. And now the punishment has been dealt to
them. Their lust has born fruit; they have actually sown the
seed of life unintentionally. What is this life? What does it
mean? What is it going to do to them? He is terrified. In his
eyes, this life which has happened so unexpectedly is a wide
and dangerous gulf, completely separating the two of them.
He feels that they have been separated by it, not realizing that
in fact this is their closest link. The sound of her crying comes
to him through the cracks and pierces his heart. His eyes are
filled with tears and his heart with hopeless pity — for her,
for himself, and for all that has happened between them. He
knows that this is the end.

She gives birth one dawn in the autumn. Everyone in the

troupe has gone to the hospital, and he is left alone, sitting in the middle of the dark, empty studio. The firm floor feels like a desert. He wraps his arms around his legs and buries his head between his knees. It is all quiet; even the insects are silent. He has become dumb; his brain refuses to function. However hard he tries he does not understand; he does not know what is going to happen; he does not know what all this means! The life has grown inside her body, and it has not shown him any new light. His blood will never mingle with its fresh young blood; he will never feel the budding and maturing of this new life, never experience the irresistable sense of responsibility and love. In fact he has made half of this new life, but still he has to try to understand it from the outside, and so the education he receives is far less profound. Besides, he is arrested by his own suffering. No help is in sight, and he is incapable of any movement. From this moment on, she has surpassed him.

She is lying in a pool of blood, in such pain that she cannot even cry out. The babies are born in this pool of blood; there are two of them, a boy and a girl.

No one who hears the babies crying one after the other will have the heart to dismiss her. A record of "serious error" is entered into her dossier and she is told that she will be the gatekeeper. A few days before she gave birth, the old gatekeeper was going to put the kettle on but collapsed half way, in the middle of the courtyard. He was dead when he was discovered. The cause of death was brain haemorrhage.

She lives with her two children in the gatehouse. Her daily duties include collecting and distributing newspapers and letters, supplying hot water and answering the telephone. It is difficult for the three of them to live on her meagre salary, and some well-meaning busy-bodies advise her that she should give one child away. But she will not hear of it because she has heard that twins must not be separated, but must be brought up together, particularly if it is a boy and a girl; if they are separated they will not live long.

Though life is difficult she feels very happy. Her heart is as peaceful as a calm lake; she has never felt so clean and pure before. The flames which had been torturing her for years have finally died down; she has actually survived her scorching desires. She feels that this has been achieved through the help of her two children, and so she is filled with gratitude and love for them, trying her best to protect them so that they will not come to any harm. Moreover, she always has this strange feeling that the children are in great danger, and that the major danger is him. She will not let him look at the children, afraid that he will strangle them just as he once tried to strangle her. She vehemently denies the relationship between the children and him.

What she does not know is that he is only mildly curious about them; even a little afraid. And yet they seem to want to attach themselves to him, growing more and more like him by the day. Their temples, noses, mouths — everyone can see that they take after him; there is no escaping the trap of a blood-tie. He can only glance at them from afar because she is always avoiding him, running away at the mere sight of him. Yet a glance is enough for him to have an impression of the children. He is surprised and frightened, because the children are trying to capture him with their own souls. He can only escape; he cannot take up the burden of this fact, the fact that he has fathered these children. No, no, they are not his; he is thoroughly unprepared; he does not understand what this means, so there is no relief for him. He is destined to go on enduring the scorching flames. And since she has escaped and he must endure it alone, the flames are burning ever more fiercely. He tries every means to find an outlet for the scorching lava inside his body.

At first he tries gambling. No one at the mahjong table is more agitated and restless than him. Eyes red, fingers twitching and legs shaking under the table, he makes the whole table rattle. He has won huge sums, and lost huge sums, including all that he has won, plus his capital and his watch. He is even in debt. And then he thinks of marriage. His family back home finds him a wife in his small home town, and in three months they are married.

**Mar.**

Life after marriage is not at all blissful for them. Every time his wife comes for a visit, she leaves before the planned date. If others ask her what is the hurry, she says tearfully that she cannot take it anymore. But she never tells anyone what it is that she cannot take, just wipes her tears and walks away. He never asks her to stay, just smiles gloomily. He has stopped practising long ago, and has taken to boozing, getting dead drunk every time. And then his kidneys are inflamed, and after that is cured he cannot very well stay with the troupe, so he is transferred to the sales counter of a department store. He feels that it is shameful for a man to stand behind a sales counter, so he returns to his home town, and his wife finds him a job in the grain control department of the town, collecting cash and coupons. On the day he leaves the troupe everyone sees him off. When he walks pass the gatehouse, she is holding a child in each arm, watching the children on the street playing five stones. Surprisingly she does not run to hide, but looks straight at him. He also fixes his eyes on her for a moment, and then he walks on.

By now they are both grown-ups, he twenty-eight, she twenty-four. Some well-wishers want to find her a husband, and she does not object; after all, being on her own all the time is really lonely. But no one is willing to take her. She is a notorious woman in this small town, a broken shoe so to speak, with two illegitimate children whose father cannot even be named. At the mere mention of her name people will spit thrice on the ground to get rid of the filth and bad luck associated with her. In fact after the baptism of lust she is cleaner and purer than at any time before, but no one understands this, not even herself; she keeps on feeling inferior. No one wants to marry her, and she does not complain, but just looks after the children and works diligently every day.

The years flow slowly by like a running stream; the stream flows by like the years. The water-men's songs have grown weaker by the day, and a water tower is built in town, pumping water directly from the river. The water-men cannot make a living now, and so their songs are silenced; no one listens to them, and no one remembers them anymore. Only on the days when the troupe has left to perform in other places, and she stays behind, alone with the children in the empty courtyard, will she hear the water-men's song, sonorous and melancholy in turn, in her peaceful dreams.

The children are growing up quickly; they can say "mama" now, and say it extremely loudly. They like playing on the faded red floor of the studio. In their eyes, it is a vast space surrounded by mirrors. When they stand in the middle, they are surrounded by themselves, and they get so scared that they run away. Yet they find it hard to suppress their curiosity, and come back hand in hand to stand fast there, watching all around. She leans against the door frame, waiting for the water to boil and holding in her hands the wooden plaque with the words "boiled water" written on it. She looks at the children rolling and crawling on the floor, and smiles sadly.

"Mama!" the children shout.

"Yes," she answers. This is a sound which can wake her from the deepest sleep.

"Mama!" the children shout again.

"Yes," she answers.

"Mama!" the children shout repeatedly, and their voices reverberate in the empty studio. It is like a voice from heaven. She feels enveloped in a sense of sacred solemnity, so she too becomes solemn.

One of Hong Kong's most distinguished writers and winner of the prestigious Taiwan **United Daily** award for fiction in 1982. Her stories reflect a haunting, often morbid, lyricism, and an intense feminine sensitivity, reacting to the unique environment of Hong Kong and its fusion of East and West, tradition and modernity. Theresa Munford writes in **The Far Eastern Economic Review** that Xi Xi is ''a writer who deserves a place in the international library.''

21.1 × 14 cm      89 pages

Yuo Luojin is one of the most outspoken women writers to have emerged in China since 1949. Her book is both an intensely personal chronicle of her experiences during the Cultural Revolution and a compelling social document.

Its harrowing account of the arrest, imprisonment and execution of the author's brother, its vivid depiction of Red Guard violence, of daily life in a labour camp, its daring portrayal of sex, have all made it one of the most widely read and controversial works of literature in contemporary China. This English translation follows the original unexpurgated text.

21.1 × 14 cm        xix + 210 pages, photos

——— *RENDITIONS* (◑|◐) *PAPERBACKS* ———

*A Chinese Winter's Tale*
By Yu Luojin

*The Old Man and Others Stories*
By Chen Ruoxi

*A Girl Like Me and Other Stories*
By Xi Xi

*Borrowed Tongue*
By Tao Yang

*Vignettes from the Chinese: Lithographs from
Shanghai in the Late Nineteenth Century*
Edited and translated by Don. J. Cohn

*A Little Primer of Tu Fu*
By David Hawkes

FORTHCOMING:

*Selected Poems*
By Gu Cheng

*Black Walls and Others Stories*
By Liu Xinwu

*Contemporary Women Writers: Hong Kong and
Taiwan*

Published by Research Centre for Translation
The Chinese University of Hong Kong
Shatin, New Territories
Hong Kong
Telephone: 0-6952399 0-6952297